UNDER HIS THUMB

CAROLYN FAULKNER

Published by Blushing Books
An Imprint of
ABCD Graphics and Design, Inc.
A Virginia Corporation
977 Seminole Trail #233
Charlottesville, VA 22901

Under His Thumb
Carolyn Faulkner

eBook ISBN: 978-1-63954-518-6
Print ISBN: 978-1-63954-519-3

Cover Art by ABCD Graphics & Design

Chapter 1

C. *1952*

That anyone knocked on her door was unusual in and of itself. And at this time of night even more so, but it was the fact that it was done so with such vehemence that caught her attention above and beyond anything else, making her already tense, small body become utterly rigid.

It had not been her experience that people who came calling at this time of night were up to any good, in general, or pertaining to herself specifically.

However, she had also learned—the hard way—that ignoring such things often led to even worse consequences, so instead of running and hiding, which was her long ingrained first instinct, Claire Beaumont stood and forced herself to walk toward the door.

Standing in front of it, not having so much as reached for the knob yet, she asked in what she hoped was a quiet, firm tone that didn't reveal her internal quavers, "Who is it?"

"You know exactly who it is, little girl," came the deep, no-nonsense reply. "Open the door."

Her automatic reaction at that all too familiar, all too

demanding tone was to bite her lip, but she knew she had to abandon any sign of nervousness around him—like not showing fear in front of a wild animal. So, she grimaced at his presumption, instead—as well she should have—at him appearing on her doorstep like this, as if she was his for the taking or some such other horribly presumptuous—and thoroughly incorrect—assumption.

"I don't think so, Mr. Ferguson. Whatever you have to say, you can say it through the door." She was thinking, "through the relative safety" of the door, but managed not to say it, especially since she knew that it was a flimsy form of protection at best.

When he finally spoke, she knew she was going to have to let him in—not because of his words, which were bad enough, but because of how he said them, in that too soft way he had that set her heart to beating fit to make it fly right out of her chest.

"You're not making the mistake of thinking that I won't bust it down, are you, Claire? I think you know me better than that, don't you?"

How could something that was said that low and soft—that downright civilly—sound so utterly threatening at the same time?

Claire knew the answer to that question before she asked it of herself, because she knew he'd do it without a second thought and just send someone from the ranch out tomorrow to fix what he'd done. No skin off his nose in the least.

With an exasperated sigh that she heartily wished had more oomph behind it, she unlocked the door without opening it then went to stand in the middle of the small living room, in what she hoped would be a defensible position, although she doubted it.

A chill went through her when he closed and locked the

door behind him, but she stood her ground, even lifting her chin as he took a step or two closer to her.

She'd forgotten just how much of a behemoth he was—or perhaps he hadn't been quite as filled out back then as he was now. Still, he was no slouch, no bumbling oaf. He was a man who was well aware of his size. He had more than enough money to buy clothes that fit his outsized frame almost too well, and he was standing in front of her in nice dress pants and an Oxford shirt with an open collar.

That said, he managed to dwarf not only her, but the entire room! Not that, on a teacher's salary, she had been able to afford the Taj Mahal, but it was more than big enough when he wasn't taking up four-fifths of it.

And he was hogging all of the air, too, it seemed to her, somehow. She was breathing quickly, as if she'd just run a race, and she knew him too well to think that he had missed that terribly revealing piece of information.

"To what do I owe the honor of this visit, Mr. Ferguson?" Claire asked, crossing her arms over her chest and staring up at him, willing herself not to look away first.

But all it took was him moving his hands to mirror her stance for her eyes to immediately dart to the worn carpet in front of the pink toes that were peeping out of her threadbare slippers.

She tightened the belt of her robe reflexively, adjusting the patch worked chenille skirt of it so that it hid from his eagle eyes what her slippers didn't, his expression so unwelcoming that she doubted she would have the guts to look up at him again.

"Don't try to play the innocent with me, Claire *Beaumont.*" He fairly spat her last name at her. "You know why I'm here. I can't believe you had the audacity to come back at all, but I'm going to make you regret that decision in any way I possibly can."

His tone was as hard as the expression on his face—solid rock, unyielding, and unfeeling.

She let herself snort at that one. "You can't possibly still be mad at me for choosing Nathan over you, can you? I didn't think you were that petty, Mr. Ferguson."

I did *think the sun rose and set on your command, at one point in my life*, she thought to herself, *but I've never thought of you as petty.*

Uncompromising, demanding, driven, yes, but generally principled.

Considering the choices that she'd made in her life, she was startled to find out that her assessment of the few men she'd allowed to get close to her was extremely flawed.

Her eyes snuck to his and were sent skittering away by his thundercloud expression for their bravery. Her feet wanted her to take a step back from him, but she stood her ground.

"Don't play dumb with me, Claire," he nearly whispered, reaching out to wrap his hand around her upper arm just tightly enough to let her know he meant business, but with a care not to hurt her that, if she had been able to think at that moment, would have surprised her. "You know what that profligate husband of yours did to me."

Her eyes found his and remained there this time, while she attempted to jerk her hand out of his grasp, but she succeeded only in hurting herself in a way that she knew would leave her with bruises.

And when she finally regained its use, Claire was excruciatingly aware that it was due to his indulgence and not her own efforts against him. "What? You mean have the audacity to marry me before you had a chance to bully me into it?"

If she'd managed to insult him—which had been her intention, despite the fact that she was the one at a distinct disadvantage—he showed no sign of it.

He was not a man used to pulling his punches, and his

barbs—when he chose to use them—were much more accurate than hers. Ruthlessness had its advantages. Even the sly, suggestive manner in which he spoke was meant to give offense, and the egotistical, slightly lopsided grin on his face only added insult to injury. "You and I know, Claire, that I wouldn't have needed to bully you in any way to have you in any way I might have wanted. I was inches away from it when you ran from me to that shadow of a man who used you up, took what you had to give, and died. I think that was the only good thing Nathan was ever able to do for you."

She didn't think. One minute, she was staring up and him and hugging herself. The next, she heard—then felt the sharp pain of—her hand connect with his chiseled jaw, which she then saw flex several times in obvious anger.

"That's your one. That's all you get. As you'll recall, I'm sure, I'm much more accustomed to being the one delivering the slaps, and if you ever strike me again, young lady, you'll need a pillow on your chair for a week afterward, I can promise you that."

Her color was high because of what she'd just done—wondering if this was the night she would meet her maker—but it rose further, nearly to the point of fainting, at his words.

"But you're not going to be around here long enough to get the opportunity to do that again, anyway."

"Of course, I am! Don't be ridiculous. I just moved here, and the school year is just beginning."

He tapped his finger against his full lips, looking thoughtful, and that just made her more worried about what he was going to say. "Yes, but I wonder what the school board would think about the fact that they're employing a woman whose husband—who I would bet is merely your fall guy—embezzled over fifty thousand dollars from me, that I intend to recover, one way or the other?" Ethan took that step he'd been denying himself since he'd entered her tiny little apartment, the one that brought him dangerously close to her.

He didn't think he'd ever know what it was about this little woman that got to him so easily, and in so many ways, few of which he was able to control. But she did. She got under his skin—bone deep—and she'd been there since he'd become aware of her when she was younger than she should have been, although he very carefully left her alone while he was in college, giving her time to graduate from high school. And become involved with that weasel she'd married instead of him. He didn't like to think of himself as egotistical, which didn't mean that he wasn't on occasion, but how she could have chosen that man instead of him was beyond his ken. Mostly, he'd tried not to think about it.

As much as parts of him definitely wanted him to—practically demanded it of him—he couldn't bring himself to go after her, so he did his best to forget her, but he wasn't very good at it at all. Several women who had done their level best to distract him, any one of whom he knew would have said yes in a minute if he'd been able to bring himself to ask them to marry him. But he hadn't been able to, and she was the reason why.

Hell, he hadn't even been able to bring himself to go after them. He felt like such a fool. They had played him for all he was worth—*she* had distracted him from his usually meticulous tendencies in regards to his business, and *he* had taken advantage of that to its fullest extent.

Ethan was in no hurry to have his own idiocy revealed to all and sundry, although he certainly knew he had the right to go after the two of them.

But now that she had decided to return to the scene of the crime, that was exactly what he intended to do. His reputation in this small town was certainly strong enough to withstand something like this—especially since he was the injured party—and he wanted his money back!

At the moment, though, she was standing there, looking all starchy like she often did, like a ruffled hen. He liked that she stood up to him. Hell, he liked it when she didn't, too. He liked most things about her entirely too much for his own comfort, but most particularly when she was like this—even though she was in the wrong—and not letting him bowl her over.

She was so small; it was as if it had never occurred to her that he was as big as he was, as if it had never come into her mind that he could have her where she stood—be inside her in a matter of seconds—and that there would be precious little she could do to stop him.

Some women had a wariness about men of his size—and demeanor, he supposed—that was born out of bad experiences with previous men.

Claire didn't have that innate caution around him, and he had always been glad that she didn't.

Most of his body would have gone along with him doing just what he was thinking of, but he refused to give in to his more prurient interests in her. He didn't want to want her that way. He didn't want Mrs. Claire Beaumont anywhere near him—or his nephew—and he was going to get rid of her one way or the other.

"I have no idea what you're talking about."

If he didn't know better, he might have been inclined to believe her.

"I don't think that that is what the School Board will think when I tell them about this at the emergency meeting I'm going to call, at which they're going to fire your pretty little behind, after which I'm going to sue you for said fifty thousand."

She blanched—physically—at that, growing visibly whiter beneath her already pale skin and wobbling a little on her feet.

Ethan automatically reached out to steady her, but she shied away from him so radically that she nearly fell, righting herself while he watched through narrowed eyes, unable to stop himself from tensing, automatically ready to help her in any way he could.

But even her staunch backbone gave way a few seconds later at what he'd said. "You…you're going to tell the School Board what?"

Steeling himself against the wispy, flimsy tone of her voice, as if she couldn't quite gather enough breath to work up any volume, he repeated, "I'm going to tell them the truth—that you and your then boyfriend stole fifty grand from me. I hope you have a contingency plan, sweetheart, because you're going to be unemployed by next Wednesday, and I'm not going to accept any sort of payment plans."

All of her puffery and all of her bravery seemed to drain out of her at that, and why the hell he felt horrible that it had, he couldn't decipher and didn't want to spend any time puzzling over. It was exactly what she should have expected from him, blithely waltzing back here like this, as if she thought he was just going to overlook what they'd done.

She should have known him better than that. She should have known better than to become entangled in such a situation at all. He certainly would never have allowed her to do so, even if he wasn't the victim.

He couldn't see Nathan as the mastermind of their little plan. That man didn't know his ass from a hole in the ground. So, over the years, when he had occasion to think—obsess—about it—about her—he had cast her in the role of instigator, even though it had been Beaumont, as one of the accountants at the firm he employed for the ranch, who'd had access to the money.

It was all at her behest; he was quite sure—even though she'd never shown any signs of being a money grubber when she was with him. In fact, more of the women he'd met after she'd left had fit that role better than she had.

But that was neither here nor there. In his mind, they were both equally responsible, and he was going to make her pay him back. He was not going to allow her to merely bat her eyes at him and talk him out of it.

This was truly the first Claire had heard about Nathan doing anything like that. Granted, when they'd gotten married, he was already quite sick, and he had insisted that he would handle their finances, such as they were.

He never took another job—he'd quickly become unable to do so—but he'd never let her get a job, either, although he did let her go to school. Where the money came from every month to pay the bills—which he saw to exclusively, too—she didn't know, but she supposed she should have asked. She did bring it up occasionally—the idea that there was a lot of money going out, but little going in, that she knew of—but he got agitated to the point of nearly becoming inconsolable when she did that, so she stopped altogether. So, she didn't push him when she apparently should have. Of course, she wasn't about to say any of that to him.

"I have no idea to what you're referring, Mr. Ferguson."

Ethan stood there, looking down at her, hands on his hips. "I should take you over my knee right here and now." Then he suited actions to words, sitting down next to her on the couch, grabbing her far wrist and tugging her over his lap, all in one smooth motion. "I'm beginning to think that just getting you fired and getting restitution isn't going to be anywhere near satisfying enough, I'm afraid. I want my pound of flesh, and I'm very happy to take it out of your hide."

Before she could draw a breath to scream at him about how highly inappropriate this was, her robe and nightgown were up around her waist, her drawers—which, like everything else she was wearing, were more hole than fabric at this point—were at her knees, and his hand was busy viciously singeing the flesh of her behind.

She never did get to take him to task for anything so mild as his impropriety. Instead, the first words that came screaming out of her mouth were for him to stop spanking her!

"I don't think so, Mrs. *Beaumont.*" Again, he emphasized her last name as if it left a bad taste in his mouth to say it.

"I'm doing for you what your husband was incapable of doing. I bet you ran roughshod over the poor man. He probably didn't know which way was up once you'd had your way with him. A woman like you can do that to man—render him senseless."

She couldn't concentrate on what he was saying—she was in too damned much pain, and trying too hard—with utter futility—to get off his lap and away from that very lethal hand of his!

"Well, maybe you could do that to a man like Nathan. But, as you know, I'm a very different kind of man. I'd never let you talk me into doing something like that, no matter how good you were in bed."

That tickled her mind a little, and she gasped in indignation, although she supposed the ship had really sailed on that, considering that she was only half dressed over his lap, getting her bottom blistered.

"I told you! I haven't got the faintest idea about Nathan embezzling anything!"

The punishment continued relentlessly, regardless of what she said or did.

And—despite how bad it was getting—she refused to give him the satisfaction of seeing her cry—although that was definitely touch and go there, especially at the end. She couldn't stop herself from trying to fight him tooth and nail —for all the good it did her—and she was screaming invectives at him as if she was trying to drive away the Devil himself. But she managed not to cry, and that was a very hard won achievement.

When his hand came down for the last time onto a bottom that by then was scarlet red and swollen and throbbing, he felt her begin to relax slowly, and he found himself wishing that he had the right to hold her now and comfort her. But he jettisoned those treasonous thoughts immediately.

That wasn't ever likely to happen, and she'd only gotten the barest slice of what she really deserved, but it was Indian Summer, and her windows were open, and he didn't fancy trying to explain to the Chief of Police why he'd been making the new schoolteacher—who he was holding half naked over his lap—scream. Rory Palmer would have had entirely too much fun ribbing him about it for the rest of his natural life.

As soon as Ethan stopped, she'd scrambled away from him—at first to cower in the corner of the couch but then deciding that was nowhere near far enough away, she shot off the couch like a rocket to the other side of the room, ending up standing just about as far away from him as she could get and still remain in the same house.

Ethan rose, too, although he did so much more slowly, heading for the door. He caught sight of her on his way, standing near the corner of the small breakfast nook in the relative darkness staring warily out at him, looking lost and forlorn.

He was again assailed by feelings and needs he had no interest in confronting, the foremost of which was a desire to pull her into his arms.

The underlying impulses were normal—he desperately wanted to fuck her, even though Beaumont had gotten there ahead of him. He had always wanted her to the point of nearly shaming himself in myriad ways, so perhaps he wasn't as different from the other man as he liked to think he was. But then again, he would never have done something illegal, no matter how much he wanted her.

Still, his arms were itching to close around her, his hands aching to rub her back or stroke her hair while she clung to him and cried.

Only, she wasn't crying now, and she hadn't cried then, which was only further proof, as far as he was concerned, of her guilt. If she felt remorse for what she had done, or if he had been spanking her and she was innocent, she would definitely have been crying.

"I'm sure you'll get an invite to the meeting, if you'd like to waste your breath trying to defend yourself. But I have all a paper trail that leads right to your husband, and since you necessarily benefited from his ill-gotten gains, you are the one I'm going to come after with everything I have."

Seconds after he closed the door, he heard something heavy crash against it.

Guess she'd gotten her nerve back.

He'd intended to go right home, but he ended up at the Round Up—the only bar in town—drinking much worse whiskey than he had at home, but for some reason, he didn't want to go there.

His dad would be sleeping, as would James, the nephew he'd adopted when his sister and her husband had died in a car accident, and whom he considered to be more of a son—especially since he was unlikely to have any other kind. There was no one waiting up for him. No one curled up, warm and welcoming and willing, beneath the warm covers of his bed.

So, he might as well stay out, for the moment, at least.

Sonny, the bartender, knew what he wanted—not that he spent all that much time there—and kept it coming.

"You seen that new schoolmarm? She's a pretty little thing. But then, she always was."

He made an unintelligible sound that didn't encourage further conversation, not that Sonny needed any such encouragement to keep talking. Ethan tapped the again empty shot glass in front of him with the side of his index finger and Sonny refilled it obligingly.

"She's going to have every eligible man in town after her as soon as they realize that she's here and available. Probably some that aren't eligible, too. We were lucky to get her on such short notice—Sally Kepler having had to stay in bed with this last pregnancy all of a sudden 'n all."

That got him to pay attention.

"What did you just say?"

"That we were lucky to get her—"

"No, before that," Ethan scowled.

Sonny grinned in a manner that Ethan took an instant dislike to. "Oh—that she was going to have every man in town after her? Why not? She may be a widow, but she's got a good job, and she's still young and cu—"

He couldn't finish his sentence because Ethan's fist found its way to his jaw in a punch that didn't seem like he'd put much power behind it but had managed to drop him to his knees anyway.

Leaving behind a huge pile of bills on the bar in apology, he left before he took that man apart piece by piece with his bare hands, thinking all the way home about what Sonny had said, and the truth behind it.

Somewhere in his sloshed brain, a light bulb went off that should have been on all of this time, and as he stumbled into his bed—after checking in on James to make sure he was all right—his arms reached out to the empty other side, as if he expected someone to be there.

That someone was miles away in the seedy but still somewhat genteel side of town, shaking with reaction and in almost the same position in which he'd left her—minus one of the butt ugly Hummels that her mother had collected and she hated that was lying shattered on the floor in front of the door through which he'd just left.

There would be no bliss of sleep for her that night, or indeed the rest of the weekend as the truth of what the big man had said sank slowly into her consciousness.

Nathan had had money he hadn't had to work for because he'd stolen from the one man in town who was the least likely to forgive and forget, especially when it came to his widow, who he seemed to think was the genius behind the whole caper.

He'd always said that he was working on some kind of big strike. She'd assumed that he meant an oil well or a stock that he thought would pay off.

And now, because she hadn't had the gumption to ask him exactly where he'd gotten the money off which they were living, she was going to lose her job and very probably go to jail, and even after that, she knew for absolute certain that Ethan Ferguson was going to hound her for the money until kingdom come.

The thought struck her that she should just leave town and not wait for the sword to fall—not that she had any misguided notions that he would leave it at that, but at least she might get some free time before she was hauled off to jail.

Do they still have debtor's prison? she wondered. But then her agile mind supplied that, if he could somehow prove that she had encouraged Nathan or knew about it—or maybe he was right when he said that, just because she had lived off the stolen money, he had the right to come after her for it, even if she was innocent. And he certainly didn't believe that she was.

It didn't really matter. Innocent or guilty, jail was jail, and destitution was destitution.

The idea of leaving had a certain amount of appeal. She hated to seem like a coward, and she supposed that she should want to stay and clear her name. But she'd have no idea how to go about doing that, nor any money with which to pay a lawyer or investigator or whoever to help her do so. Claire had no idea where she would go, either.

And if she left like this, with no notice, she wouldn't be able to use Lincoln School as a reference. She'd have a hard time getting another teaching job, without one, which was her best bet at steady employment that wasn't something part time and low wage, like waitressing.

Something like this was quite likely to follow her wherever she went, with or without Ethan's sense of vengeance. She might not end up in prison—she certainly didn't deserve to—but she could certainly end up penniless and living on the streets, begging for money or… worse. Much, much worse.

It was highly unlike her, but she felt frozen and had no idea what to do. She'd done the best she could after Nathan had died. By then, the money—whoever it belonged to—was long gone, and she had been living hand to mouth, tutoring and substitute teaching occasionally, while taking care of him.

When he was gone—other than realizing with a certain amount of horror that she wasn't all that sorry to have seen him go—she set about trying to rebuild her life, and finding a job as a teacher was the biggest step in that.

She'd thought that, finally, her life was coming together. It was going to be what she'd wanted it to be originally, before she'd let Nathan talk her into essentially running away with him.

But now, Claire didn't know which way to turn. Living away from Somerset, her home town, with her husband, who wasn't the most social of beings, had isolated her. Her family was gone, and so were her friends, or at the very least, they had grown away from her. She had just barely gotten back into town, so she hadn't had a chance to re-establish those relationships at all.

As a result, Claire spent most of the weekend, until late Sunday afternoon, hovering in the corner of her worn couch, crouched there, holding herself, hunkering down and huddling up as if she was caught outside in a blizzard, not feeling anything, and not thinking anything.

Especially nothing about him.

Chapter 2

IT WASN'T until late Sunday afternoon that Claire was able to mentally shake herself by the shoulders and do something, rather than just sitting around, struck dumb and numb.

She still hadn't cried about the relatively hopeless situation in which she'd found herself, and forcing herself to do something made that an even less likely prospect. She was too stunned to break down like that at the moment, although she knew there was going to be time enough for it when there was nothing else to concentrate on.

Although she was still uncertain about where it was that she was going to end up, she knew that—regardless—she was going to need to get packed. If she actually went through with it and left, she'd have to stiff her landlord, with whom she had signed a lease, which she hated to do. Mrs. Harrington was the quintessential little old lady, warm and loving and dear, and her income from renting this apartment —which was above the store her family had owned at one time—was what she relied on to get by. But that couldn't be helped.

When she needed to be, Claire could be organized and

methodical. It didn't come naturally to her—she leaned more toward the artistic, which she relied on a lot while teaching. And it helped that she hadn't been here very long, so she wasn't completely unpacked. In fact, the tiny second bedroom, which was really not much more than a closet, was still full of boxes and bags she hadn't yet gotten to.

The physical activity of packing was good for her, though. It kept her mind occupied. She wasn't anywhere near as careful in doing so as she had been in getting her stuff here, but time was more of the essence in this situation than it had been.

She hadn't eaten much all weekend, and she wasn't bothering to do so now, either, since she was finally able to do what she needed to do. She felt that if she didn't get this done while she was feeling as if she could, it would never get done. Claire allowed it to absorb every bit of her, packing and moving each box as she was finished with it into the living room, although she was careful to leave clear paths back and forth.

Thus, when there was yet another knock at the door in the late evening, she was so preoccupied that it made her jump worse than the first one had. And she was made even more nervous by the fact that she was even more certain—this time—of who it was, and that she definitely didn't want to see him.

Hell, she was still sitting—when she forgot and did so—very gingerly as a result of his last visit! So, she dispensed with the games about not knowing who was on the other side and stood in front of her own front door again, drawing a deep breath and trying to gird her loins as best she could.

"Yes, Mr. Ferguson?" Unfortunately, it didn't come out with the bravado that it had in her mind. In fact, it sounded as exhausted as she felt.

"Let me in."

Her weary mind got all whimsical at that, picturing most definitely as a very big, very bad wolf.

Claire had neither the time nor the inclination to fight with him, so she unlocked her door and went back to packing.

"Going somewhere?" he asked, leaning casually up against the bookshelf by the door and crossing his arms over his chest.

Those muscles might have been distracting at any other time, but she was trying to continue to be as single minded as she had been and get things done.

"You know that won't alleviate your problem."

"Yes, it will," she returned smartly. "I'll be miles and miles away from you."

Ethan frowned at that. "You don't think I'll come after you?" he asked, not bothering to conceal the blatant threat.

"Of course, you will," she answered matter-of-factly. "I'm surprised you didn't do so before."

"So am I," he murmured under his breath. Then he took a step toward her, relieving her of the handful of books she was trying to pack neatly away. "Stop packing. You're not going anywhere."

"You can't stop me." She turned to stare up at him bravely.

Bravely? Stupidly? She honestly couldn't tell anymore. Her life was in such turmoil since he'd left that she didn't know which way was up. Running away was the only thing she could think of to do besides sit there and wait to see the blue lights flashing outside her window.

One eyebrow rose nearly to his hairline. "You've never been stupid, Claire. Don't start now."

She continued packing even more furiously than before, as if her life depended on it, and until he literally forced her to sit down on the couch.

"I can't really believe I'm saying this, but you don't have to leave. And I won't say anything to the Board."

In different circumstances, he might have laughed out loud at the suspicious look she gave him.

"Forgive me if I'm skeptical of your change of heart. It's not like you to do anything altruistic."

Just his frown was more than enough to make her shiver. "I didn't go after you, did I?"

"No, you didn't," she agreed, throwing caution to the wind and saying exactly what she was thinking. What the hell? Why not? She was probably going to end up in jail anyway. "But I have a feeling that was more a matter of wanting to save face since I chose Nathan over you rather than not wanting to prosecute the ever-loving crap out of him."

Claire watched the big man draw a slow, deep breath and wondered if she'd gone too far.

"Out of the both of you, little girl. The both of you. You'll never, ever convince me that you were innocent. You're too smart, and he was too stupid by far."

"You underestimate him. You always did."

He chuffed. "Blaming your dead husband, Claire? Really?"

She knew she wasn't going to get anywhere with him by declaring her innocence. He didn't want to hear or know anything she might say about it.

"Why are you here—again—Mr. Ferguson?"

He looked… she wasn't sure how he looked, but it wasn't a usual expression for him. That was until he noticed that she was scrutinizing him, and then he presented her with his usual angry face.

"I'm here because I want something from you that I should have had back then."

What could that be? she wondered but wasn't about to ask.

"All of this will go away—well, at least, there will only be two of us that know about it. I won't tell the board. You won't lose your job—although I won't allow you to get another one when Sally comes back. No running away, no bad reputation, no jail time. No payback—at least," his grin was the epitome of evil intent, "not in a monetary sense, anyway."

Claire snorted. "Yeah, I can't see that any of that is likely to happen, especially considering what you were saying to me about forty-eight hours ago."

"I know. I've had some time to think, and I have a better solution than throwing you in jail. You're really no good to me there. You can't even pay me back from there, although that goal has been sidelined for the greater good in favor of this plan, which I have to admit that I much prefer."

She sighed tiredly. "Just for shits and giggles, and knowing that I probably don't want to hear this, either, what is your new plan for ruining my life?"

That scowl was formidable, although she didn't really know why he would wear one. Did he not realize that he was going to ruin her life, no matter what he decided to do? Maybe he didn't, since he certainly didn't care.

That was when she realized that he had, slowly but surely, gotten much too close to her. And he proceeded to show her, rather than tell her, what he intended.

The moment his lips met hers, it was as if the past few years had never happened. They were still dating, and it was absolutely explosive between them, so much so that she had felt she had to tell him that she was not going to sleep with him on their very first date.

To his credit, he'd been insulted that she'd felt she needed to say that. "I want you, have no doubt about it, sweetheart. But I have never forced myself on a lady, and I'm not going to start with you."

He didn't, although she knew it was damned close for him at times, as it was for her, too. They were two combustible substances which, when mixed, became downright nuclear.

His lips were demanding, as they'd always been. Although he definitely made sure that she was enjoying what he was doing, he wasn't the type of man to ask permission. He expected—and received—a response from her, and at first, it was quite encouraging.

It had been so long since she'd been touched like this that Claire felt as if she was drowning in the kind of sensuality he was so easily able to conjure in her. It was just like she remembered—overwhelming, a little frightening, but terribly hot at the same time.

But then she realized what he meant by doing this. He was going to expect her to pay him back with her body, and she wasn't about to do that.

She began to struggle against him, and it was all Ethan could do to convince himself to let her go. He'd largely forced himself to forget how incredible it felt to hold her in his arms, how warm and soft she was pressed up against his chest like that, lips opening beneath his like a flower to the sun.

When she was free, she took up that spot again in the dining room again, looking at him warily as he ran his hand impatiently through his wavy hair and began to pace.

"I will not sleep with you to pay some imaginary debt you've decided that I owe you."

"It's not imaginary, Claire."

"I'd rather go to jail first."

His chuckle was completely mirthless. "You wouldn't last a week, sweetcakes. Really. They would eat you up, and not in a good way."

She looked as befuddled by that remark as she would have been before she left.

What kind of lover had that waste of humanity Nathan been to her, anyway? How could any red-blooded man not put his mouth all over her, most especially *there*?

"I am your nephew's teacher. This is a very small town. People will talk. And if they do, then I'll lose my job anyway. You might as well just go ahead and tell them." She sighed again, and this time it was bone deep. "It doesn't really matter, one way or the other."

Every word she'd said was right. He hadn't bothered to look past his aching hard on to the consequences of his actions, of getting what he desperately wanted—much more so than the money—which he didn't like one bit. Ethan prided himself on being logical; he looked at every angle of every problem. But not in this case, apparently. He'd let his genitals have their way instead.

She'd turned away from him, shoulders slumped in on themselves, seeming just that much smaller and more helpless, although he saw no signs that she was crying.

If she wanted to elicit sympathy from him, she should have been turning on the waterworks. Isn't that what most women did when they wanted to get their own way? Not that that was going to deter him in the least. But it surprised him quite a bit that she was so dry eyed. In fact, she hadn't cried the last time he was here, either, despite the fact that he'd tanned her hide but good, besides delivering the news that she wasn't going to get away with stealing from him.

Somehow, that didn't sit well with him, although he couldn't put his finger on why. It certainly was easier not to have to deal with a woman who was sobbing hysterically. But still, it felt wrong to him, somehow.

But he wasn't going to dwell on it. Instead, he turned toward her and said what had popped into his mind before he had a chance to think too hard about what a terrible idea it was, again acting against type and in favor of his distinctly carnal interest in her, which seemed to be overriding his common sense all over the place in regards to her.

"Then we'll get married."

Silence.

He waited a long moment then flipped the light on so that he could see her better.

Oh, God. Here comes the sobbing, he thought, when he saw her shoulders moving quickly up and down. Unlike a lot of men, though, he was brave enough to walk toward the storm, rather than away from it. If he had been willing to examine his motives further—which he wasn't—he would have realized that he was looking forward to the opportunity to comfort her, even if it really was just another way of getting to hold her.

But when Ethan reached Claire, and she let him turn her around, toward his waiting arms, he discovered that she wasn't crying. She was laughing, just as hysterically as she might have been crying. There were tears streaming down her cheeks but not from sadness.

She walked right by him, holding her hand over her mouth and her arm around her own middle as she bent over with the force of her amusement.

As he watched her and let her get it out of her system, Ethan stood there like a statue. A very unhappy statue.

When she finally recovered the power of speech, Claire wiped her eyes, continuing to chuckle a bit as she did so. "Ahh, haa, haa! That is rich! Marry you!" She was off into gales of laughter again, ignoring how angry he looked. "I wouldn't marry you if you were literally the last man on Earth."

"You'd rather lose your job? Have your reputation ruined?" he listed off in a deathly quiet tone. "End up in jail and still owe me even when you get out? Hmm. I don't think they let felons teach school, do you?"

That sobered her up faster than anything else he could have said.

She loved teaching, and she was damned good at it. It was the one thing she'd always wanted to do in her life—above marrying and even having children of her own. She loved the idea of being independent, running her own classroom, introducing the kids to new things, helping them learn, and hopefully cultivate, a lifelong love of reading. To say nothing of having summers off to travel if she wanted to.

All of that was gone now, she realized with a start. All because of Nathan. No, she revised. No one had forced her to marry him. No one had held a gun to her head. She had made her own bed, and she'd lain down in it, too, without asking whose money had paid for it. Granted, she hadn't known about her husband's perfidy.

But she had to own up to the fact that she was the one who had fled from the incredible intensity of what she felt for Ethan—not to mention what she suspected he felt for her. He was a powerhouse, and she had begun to feel very overwhelmed by him. Nathan was so light and breezy and casual and relaxing, in comparison.

Of course, he didn't make her feel like Ethan did—he didn't even attempt to—but that was a plus at times, to not be the object of such intensity all the time.

And Nathan didn't spank her, either. She didn't think that idea would have ever so much as entered his head.

It was certainly set in Ethan's. He had spanked her frequently, each time to well beyond the point at which she had begun crying. If she was honest with herself, which she did try to be, she had to admit that he'd never done so for what could be considered a frivolous reason. It had only ever been that he felt she had shorted herself in some way—not taken care of herself or put herself in harm's way.

Still, that didn't negate the fact that they were terribly painful. Although she certainly had liked the way he'd soothed her afterward.

While she mulled over ancient history and events she couldn't change, Ethan was watching her carefully. At least she wasn't laughing anymore. But she'd gone away from him, somehow, and he didn't much care how. He wanted her there, with him, and he wanted her to agree to do what he wanted.

Ethan gave her shoulders a little shake, waiting until her eyes focused on his before he spoke.

"Think about it, Claire. You're a smart girl, maybe a bit too smart for your own good, but then, I always did know how to curb that in you, didn't I?"

She thought he was going to kiss her again, but instead, he took a step away from her.

"I want your answer by Tuesday night. I'll come back then."

He made his way to the door, pausing there to throw back over his shoulder, "And don't try to leave town. You know I'll find you, and that'll just make me angrier than I already am."

When he left, she fell to her knees, remaining there until her body began to cramp up in protest. Then, without doing or thinking another thing, just following her body's dictates, she headed for her bedroom and crawled under the covers, barely able roust herself when the alarm went off that meant she needed to get ready for school.

The question of whether or not she'd go never entered her mind. She wanted to go, so she was going. Teaching was the only thing in her life that gave her pleasure, and she was loathe to give it up—hence the fact that she hadn't left yesterday, right after he did.

Claire had absolutely no idea what she was going to do or say when he arrived on her doorstep yet again tomorrow night. But for now, she was a teacher, and she was going to damned well teach.

But even the thought of spending the day with those thirty eager minds wasn't enough that morning to put any kind of a smile on her face.

Her fellow teachers noticed. Gloria Teta, who was the teacher of the other third grade class, frowned at her. "Don't tell me you're getting that deadly flu that's going around, too. You look like death warmed over."

Claire summoned a wan smile. "You're always so complimentary, Gloria," she teased.

Gloria flushed but grinned. "Sorry. I plead lack of manners due to only having had brothers. What can I say?" She put her hand on the other woman's arm. "But you do look bad. I can combine our classrooms if you need to take the rest of the day off?"

Oh, God, staying at home with nothing to do but perseverate about how her life was in a tailspin was her idea of hell at the moment. She was sure that Ethan—given the chance—could concoct many more of them, though, each one worse than the other.

"No, but thank you. I'm just a little tired."

Even the kids noticed and were unusually well behaved as a result.

At lunchtime, when she was doing her playground duty, little Melissa Broadturn brought her the remains of her half-eaten apple "to cheer her up".

The sweetest of all, though, ironically, was James Norton, the nephew of the man who was determined to ruin her life.

He followed her around, occasionally presenting her with a flower—a dandelion, since those were the only ones around—and telling her bad jokes to try to get her to laugh. When the bell rang, she hugged him to her and thanked him for all of his efforts at making her feel better.

"Did it help?" he asked, brightening hopefully.

"Yes, it did," she reassured him. "I feel much better now. Thank you!"

He positively beamed at that, running off to join the line to go into the building.

How could that child be such a sweetie, and his uncle, who had, she was learning, ended up raising him when his parents died, was such a bastard?

When the bell rang again at three, Gloria appeared in her doorway. "Hey, we're all headed to Margaret's house for a coffee klatch. Wanna come?"

"Oh, I don't know. I have a lot of work to do."

"Honey, take it from me. I've been teaching for ten years. There'll always be a lot of work to get done. Do it tonight, and come out and have some harmless fun. You look as if you could use it."

Claire still hesitated, prompting Gloria to ask, "Unless you're not feeling well enough. In which case, don't let me push you into it. I just know some of the girls would love to get to know you."

Making a split-second decision to go—just to not have to go back to her apartment for once—Claire stood. "But I didn't bring anything."

"You don't need to. Margaret loves to bake, and she'll

have enough stuff to feed the third army. And how could you have known to make something when you've never been? Just go and enjoy. Margaret makes the best cinnamon rolls you've ever tasted."

She didn't have much of an appetite, which everyone seemed to notice and comment on. She had never been told by so many people in one place at one time that she needed to gain weight.

"A stiff wind would knock you over. Eat, girl!" Margaret didn't have to deal with that particular problem, and she proceeded to load Claire's plate with all sorts of sweets and goodies that she knew she wasn't going to come anywhere near finishing.

"Coffee or coffee?" Terri Martin, who was the principal, asked, holding up two pots.

"What's the difference?"

"One is regular coffee. One is high test; it's got a little something extra in it." She winked.

"Regular coffee, I think." She wasn't much of a drinker, and she didn't think she wanted to start becoming one in front of her boss.

Everyone was very nice and very welcoming. All of them were older and more experienced than she was—even the newest there had been teaching for five years, and they all—to a woman—offered any kind of assistance she might need, from how to run the cantankerous mimeograph machine to old lesson plans she could rework, to decorations for her classroom, all of which she could definitely use.

"There's no telling when Sally will be back. I guess there was a bit of a complication, and she may need to take more time to recover than she'd originally thought."

"Honestly, I can't understand why she's coming back at all. It's not like Jack can't support her. Why does she need to work?"

"Because it feels great to do something outside the home, and a woman can be more than a wife and a mother."

She'd never felt so many sets of censorious eyes on her, until Gloria chuckled and said, "It's so cute that you feel that way! You'll change your mind, though, when you meet the right man. You'll be perfectly happy to stay home and take care of him and your eventual children."

The others agreed, and someone whose name she didn't remember chimed in with, "Although there aren't a lot of eligible males around Somerset."

Everyone nodded in agreement.

"Yeah, but there's still Ethan Ferguson."

All of the women sighed as if they were bobby-soxers and he was Frank Sinatra.

She didn't join them in that and even managed to keep her mouth shut about just how much her opinion of the man differed from theirs.

Claire had to wonder why Sally didn't feel that way. And, since she didn't, and by that logic, whether, maybe Jack wasn't the right man for her.

But she didn't say any of that. She didn't know—realistically—for how much longer she'd have this job, and she didn't want to alienate anyone while she did.

She was just going to savor every bit of whatever time she had left to do it—including this part of it—until it ended in an ugly scene of some sort, inevitably instigated by her nemesis—and their dreamboat——for one made up reason or another.

That evening, she tried to devote herself to correcting spelling and math papers as well as working on the small essay about their families that she had the children working on, but she was terribly distracted. Not even watching *I Love Lucy* or *Burns and Allen* on one of the few things she'd retained from her marriage—a twelve inch Motorola television—

could engage a mind that was whirling furiously, looking for a way out of her predicament but not finding one.

And desperately trying not to think about what it might be like to be married to a man she should, by all rights, hate with a limitless passion. And she did—well, most of her did, anyway.

Only, it was that very different kind of passion that she was preoccupied by when she least wanted to be, once she'd crawled into bed and was alone with her thoughts. She'd thought she was so exhausted, mentally and physically, that she'd just drop off. Instead, her mind was flooded with unwanted thoughts of him. Ethan kissing her, Ethan spanking her, Ethan pressing the fingers of a surprisingly tender hand beneath her panties so that he could feel how wet she was.

"Oh my God, peach!" he'd breathed almost reverently that night, while they were curled up on the couch at the ranch. "You're sopping wet!"

Claire had blushed brightly, glad that the lights were down low so he couldn't see, although it wasn't as if he didn't know that she was an utterly untouched virgin until he came along. Her hand was already on his wrist—not that she had any illusions that she could stop him from doing anything he wanted to do to her, but more as a reminder of her ignorance of such matters. He knew that new things—new experiences—could be frightening for her.

But he'd always been very gentlemanly and respectful with her in the first place, and when it came to the intimacies he was slowly introducing her to, he responded immediately any time she voiced a concern about what he was doing.

And when Ethan began to move his hand upward from where it had been baptized so generously, gently and carefully opening lips that had never before been touched by a man, she exerted more pressure, and he stopped.

"I-I thought you were just going to check," she had whispered, eyes darting to and then away from his dark ones.

"Yes, I was." He swallowed so hard, she heard him do it. "But there's one more thing I'd like to do, honey, and then I'll take my hand away entirely. Trust me just a little bit more, baby."

It wasn't really a question, but it was uttered with such sincerity that she had to nod her head, even though she was practically vibrating in his arms, beset by a potent mixture of nerves, fear, and desire.

"Thank you," he'd murmured, kissing her cheek innocently as his fingers found what they had been looking for, slipping slickly over a clit that was more than ready for his touch.

She'd groaned then in a way she never had before in a rare, unguarded moment, and the raw, unfettered sound of it brought the blood to settle heavily in a place on his person that was already throbbing and stiff with it. He'd then dragged them slowly over her, and she groaned again as she remembered what he'd done to her.

And the fact that he'd held fast to his promise—removing his hand immediately once he'd stirred her up in the most intimately aching manner possible, arranging the waistband of her demure white briefs, then zipping up her skort, despite the fact that she was undulating and writhing against him, desperate for more of his touch—only made her both trust him more and wish he'd given her reason not to.

She'd been out of her mind at that moment and would have given him anything he'd asked for if he'd just put his hand back where it had been and kept it there for a while. How long, she wasn't sure, but long enough to accomplish… something. Something big, she was certain of it.

Claire had even gone so far as to grab his hand and try to

pull it back to her, but he just tilted his head a little and gave her a look that had her instantly letting go.

"But, Ethan!" she'd whimpered, hating to sound as if she was whining, or desperate, or, worse than either of those things—downright loose.

He had chuckled deeply, seemingly unaffected by her plight.

"No, sweetheart. I told you there was only one more thing I was going to do, and I don't want you doubting my word, just like I don't want you thinking I'm not going to spank you again if you keep whining, which I definitely will, even though you just got your little fanny tanned for sassing me not five minutes ago."

That had her withdrawing from him completely, looking aghast at the thought. From early on in their relationship, he had been the one in control, watching over her and correcting her in the worst possible way whenever she did something he thought she oughtn't. She'd been spanked more than enough by him for it to work as the deterrent he had intended. Claire could live quite happily without ever being spanked by him again.

But she blushed again, remembering that one of the reasons he had wanted to touch her there was to prove to her that, as much as she protested that she didn't, her body loved it when he disciplined her.

As she lay in her lonely bed, lost in her own memories, Claire ached with a need that had never been satisfied.

"You've never let that idiot Nathan do anything like that to you, have you?" he'd asked, his tone casual, but his body was tense, and she had a feeling that the answer meant more to him than he was willing to let on.

She had shaken her head solemnly. "No, I haven't." She didn't reveal that Nathan had never so much as tried to kiss her, though, much less put his hand down her pants. She wasn't sure why she kept things like that to herself. Perhaps it was because she thought big man on campus, college graduate Ethan Ferguson was just the slightest bit full of himself and that she didn't want him to think he didn't have any competition for her affections.

Years later, Claire admitted to herself that was exactly why she hadn't told him. It wasn't any of his business, either, and she shouldn't have betrayed a confidence that was between Nathan and herself, but she definitely wasn't altruistic enough to have had either of those reasons in mind.

No, she had wanted to make him jealous, to poke the bear a bit. He was so damned self-confident and self-assured that she figured the existence of a rival might take him down a peg or two.

Dammit. Even now, she wanted him. She always had. That made the decision he was forcing her to make just that much worse than it might have been if there hadn't been this rampant attraction on both sides. It would have been so much more cut and dried if her body wasn't firmly in his camp.

Claire pressed her thighs together and rolled onto her side, hoping that would help sleep come to her.

But one big question kept dancing around her head till the wee hours of the morning. What was she going to do?

Chapter 3

INSTEAD OF HIM knocking demandingly on her door this time, he was waiting for her when she got home. That didn't make her any happier, frankly, not that he was likely to ask her opinion.

She lived in a part of town where she didn't think any of the other teachers lived, but still. She really wasn't happy with the idea that someone could have seen him. Claire supposed that that was a stupid reaction, given their situation. Whether or not he was seen coming or going from her house really was irrelevant if she was going to be fired tomorrow anyway.

And she still hadn't decided whether that was the route she was going to take—although she could hardly countenance his other suggestion.

Marry him? Not likely.

Honestly, she thought she'd be happier just sleeping with him, she was astonished to realize. At least then, she wouldn't be tied to him forever.

When she drove her beat-up car into the space next to

his, he was at her door to open it for her. Claire got out and headed for her apartment, but he caught her arm.

"Come with me. I want us to go to a more private place to talk."

"But—"

One thing she could say about him, he never ignored her. Whether or not she was saying something he liked, he always paid attention to her when she said something. His responses weren't always what she might have hoped for—especially when she ended up getting spanked—but Nathan had a tendency to just pretend that she hadn't spoken, or he hadn't heard her, when he was standing right next to her.

At least Ethan didn't do that.

Of course, she could have done without him looking down at her from beneath heavily drawn brows until she sighed and turned back to him, knowing it was useless to try to argue with him.

But she did look pointedly at where his hand held her arm, just above her elbow, then up at him, and back to his hand again pointedly, and he—reluctantly—let her go. That definitely gave her a bit of a thrill, even if it was rather like getting away with hurling a rock at a lion. He'd scowled at her as she'd moved away from him, and she knew she would have to be careful when she got in little digs like that not to go too far—by *his* standards, not hers.

He was very patient with her—or he had been, before—and she had thought she had gotten to know him well enough to judge just how far she could push him.

But every once in a while, he proved to her that she didn't. She'd given him the right to spank her—if only tacitly—and he had definitely availed himself of the opportunity when she would have sworn that he wasn't going to, just to teach her the lesson that he could, she suspected. Now, all bets were off. She didn't feel as if she knew him at all, considering what he was doing to her, so it probably didn't behoove her to challenge him. But she wasn't at all sure that she could be the type of person that didn't.

They ended up at the ranch. She'd been there a couple of times before, but not often.

"Dad has taken James to a baseball game in the city. They won't be back until late tonight," he explained on the way in.

He'd opened her door for her, but she'd refused the hand he'd offered to her. Claire had been careful not to walk too close to him, either, lest he try to put his arm around her waist, and he was beginning to look like a thundercloud at the way she was so blatantly avoiding him, but she ignored him—at her own peril, she acknowledged to herself.

It looked much the same as it had before. It had a very different design from any house she'd ever been in. The main part of the house was very open—the big, country style kitchen flowed into a dining area, but somehow it still managed to retain a bit of formality to it. Perhaps it was the long dining table, as if the person who had decorated it had anticipated having a large family with lots of kids. But it, too, was all open to the living room, where there were several big comfortable, inviting looking couches and easy chairs, all gathered cozily around a big fireplace. There was also a small TV in the corner of the room, but it was obviously an afterthought.

"Can I get you anything?" he asked solicitously

Clair hugged her arms around herself. "No, thank you."

As he suppressed the urge to pull her into his arms, Ethan suggested instead, "Why don't you sit down?"

"Thank you, but I'd prefer to stand."

He grimaced at that, but he didn't say anything. She seemed determined not to relax, and in a way, he could understand that. He wasn't very often nervous or on edge, but he was both at the moment, waiting for her to tell him what she was going to do.

"So. Have you come to a decision?"

Although she would have said that she had no idea what she was going to say to him when she opened her mouth, she knew as soon as she said the words that her choice was the right one—in no small part due to the fact that they seemed to annoy him quite considerably.

"First of all, I want you to know that I will never forgive you for putting me into this position. I'm not going to protest my innocence to you again, because I know you've already made up your mind against me, and nothing I say will change it, so I won't waste my breath or your time. I just wanted to make sure that you realize that my agreeing to do this in no way means that I am conceding that I'm guilty, because I'm not."

Claire didn't look at him, nor did she wait for him to reply.

"And I've changed my mind." She watched his eyes roll then said, "It's a woman's prerogative. As I have less than no interest in marrying again—certainly not to you—and since you are determined to have, as you've said, your pound of flesh, I would prefer it if we simply had an affair. It'll take a bit of doing to make sure that we're not caught, but that's more than worth it to me so that I'll be free at some point in the end."

Ethan opened his mouth to say something, but she barged ahead, not giving him the chance.

"And that brings me to a stipulation I have about it."

His mouth closed and his eyebrows rose comically at her declaration. "A stipulation? I hardly think that you're in a place to be dictating anything, Mrs. Beaumont."

"Nevertheless, if I was to pay you off with money, there would be set payments of certain amounts. There would be a start date and an end date, assuming I met all the payments. I'm not about to allow this thing to just be open ended and go on forever. So, since this was your idea originally, not to mention that you have the means to do so, I want you to engage a lawyer who will draw up an agreement between us—a certain number of assignations over a certain number of months or years." She added softly and with a great deal of reluctance, "Enough so that you agree that they would be equal to the sum you think I owe you."

"You *do* owe me," he ground out, not at all happy about how this was going so far.

Claire counted it as a personal victory that her voice, as well as her expression, was carefully neutral, unlike his. "Yes, well, we need to assign a value to… to what you expect me to do, so that we can determine for just how long I have to do it. I'm sure a lawyer could draw something up for us once we arrive at that figure."

"How could I possibly know what value to put on an experience that I've never had?"

She couldn't control the blush that suffused her cheeks, but she could ignore it as much as possible, forging painfully ahead while desperately trying to maintain a distance from the subject they were skirting around. "Perhaps you're right. Perhaps you wouldn't find me pleasing in the least—I hadn't thought about that."

She was frowning fiercely now, and he took the time to look at her—really look at her. She was something. Ethan could hardly believe that they were having this discussion about how many times she was going to sleep with him over the course of who knew how many years, such that it would equal, what was—to anyone—a very large sum of money.

It all sounded entirely too vague and nebulous to him. Although he'd been surprised to hear it come out of his mouth when it had, the more he'd thought about it, the more the idea of marrying her had grown on him. She'd be his wife, to do with as he pleased. He liked the propriety of it, and if he was willing to admit it to himself—and he wasn't—he liked the permanence of it very much, too.

She wouldn't be able to disappear at the end of it. She would be his, always. For some reason, that appealed to him enormously, much more so than sneaking around trying to hide the relationship and inevitably getting caught, because with small towns like theirs, that always happened. Someone knew someone who knew someone who had seen something, and before they even knew they'd been spotted, everyone would be talking about them.

"And I want it as a part of the contract that you'll make every effort to keep this a secret, and I get to keep my job throughout—dependent on my performance, of course."

Just one eyebrow remained up as he looked at her expectantly. "Anything else? Would you like my lawyer to draw up your will while I have him around?"

She straightened her back at his sarcasm, answering the question as if it was a serious one. "No, thank you. I don't have much, and everyone who's getting something already knows what they're getting."

He dragged his hand down over his face then said, "Let me see if I've got this straight. In exchange for cancelling your fifty-thousand-dollar debt to me—"

"Which I do not acknowledge having and you are blackmailing me into repaying…" she interjected, although she trailed off at the end in consideration of the look he was giving her.

"I, I'm assuming, get the privilege of paying for us to stay somewhere, anywhere, outside of town as if we were high schoolers trying to put one over on our parents? So, I essentially have to schedule a time and spend my own money to fuck you every once in a while, when *you* owe *me*?"

She shrugged, refusing to allow him to upset her. "Well, it's not like I expect you to take me to a Hilton. I'm fine with some no-tell motel somewhere. I just would like it to be away from town, preferably well away from town."

She could see that that had not made things better as far as he was concerned.

"No. I'm not going to sneak around to have you. For that amount of money, I want you at my beck and call, seven days a week, twenty-four hours a day. And the only way to get that is to marry you, so I am willing to make that sacrifice."

"Well, I am not," Claire stated as she felt her mouth go dry with nerves at the way this was going—or rather, not going. "I don't want to be tied to you—a man who obviously hates me—for the rest of my life."

He looked surprised—and almost insulted—by her characterization of how he felt about her, but what else was she supposed to think? That he loved her while treating her this way?

But she was too involved in her own shame and misery to notice.

"I don't want to be married to anyone, frankly. I just want to be left alone to teach. That's all I've ever really wanted."

"You wanted me at one point—at quite a few points, as I recall," he countered.

And she blushed full on.

"That's not the same thing."

"And Nathan gave you better than I did in that department, apparently, since you chose him. Were you ever really a virgin while you were with me, or were you letting him have you and stringing me along the whole time?"

"Yes, Ethan, that was exactly what I was doing. I was sleeping with Nathan while I bilked you out of how many furs? How many diamonds? How many fancy dinners?"

She felt a lot of satisfaction at the way his face pinched up at that, because they both knew that he hadn't done any of those things for her. He might have been the heir to the richest family around these parts—even then—but she would never have expected any of those things from him. Hell, the most expensive date they'd ever had was dinner at a little home-style restaurant in town, or perhaps the time he took her to the movies in another town.

She frowned up at him. "I knew that was what this was about. You're jealous of Nathan."

His face closed up at that. "What this is about is me getting my money—or something of value to me over time—back. And sneaking around having an affair is off the table. So, you need to decide—now—whether or not you want to go to jail."

He stood there, with his hands on his hips, looking as if he wouldn't wait forever for her answer, either.

Despite the brave front she was trying to maintain, Claire felt trapped, and all of this tension and pressure was making her feel lightheaded, as if she was going to faint.

She almost swooned, and he lunged toward her, but she sucked it up, avoiding his touch and turning away from him to stand on her own.

Ethan remained on alert, ready to catch her if she fell. He wished she'd sit down already!

He heard her take a deep breath, only to sigh it slowly out seconds later, sounding as if she was going to be facing a firing squad rather than agreeing to marry him.

"All right, but I have conditions."

Both her capitulation and the elation he felt at it were a surprise to him, but he kept those facts carefully cloaked. He felt parts of himself relax in a way they hadn't done since he'd found out she was in town again. "Again, let's revisit the idea that you're in no place to make demands, peach."

Claire whirled around and met his eyes. "Then I guess I'm going to jail."

She looked gloriously defiant, and he knew how stubborn she could be. He hadn't been kidding when he'd said to her that he didn't think she'd last a week in jail, and because of that, he knew that he would do almost anything to avoid letting it happening.

"What do you want?" he ground out in a tone that let her know that whatever she was going to say was the last thing he wanted to hear.

Claire knew that he was quite likely to veto anything she said, just on general principles.

"I want to be able to keep my job."

"Okay."

"And if Sally Kepler comes back, I want to look for another more permanent one."

He seemed less enamored with that idea, so it took him a minute to finally agree. "All right, I suppose."

"I'm assuming that if I'm living with you, you'll supply room and board?"

That got her a dark look. "Of course, although your room will also be mine."

Claire's eyes wandered from his at the stark reality of that concept, but then she pushed it to the back of her mind while doing some quick mental calculations. If she got a full-time job as a first-year grade school teacher, she could expect to make about three thousand dollars a year, of which she'd actually take home about twenty-three hundred or so.

Then she extrapolated from there and wished she hadn't. Even if she was able to get a full-time job at that rate, it would still take her over twenty years to pay him off, and that was giving him every red cent she made!

"Then I want four fifths of my salary to go to you, to pay toward this fictitious debt."

He looked absolutely dumbfounded that she would require that, but a thought struck him and he came to stand in front of her, tipping her chin up with a curled finger beneath it, so that he was staring down into her eyes.

"In fact, I'll go so far as to say that if you'll admit to me right now that you owe me this money, I'll forgive half of it."

Ten years tied to him, give or take, in her mind, if she'd admit that she'd done something—not just something, but committed a felony—that she hadn't.

Ethan really wasn't presenting her with any kind of choice at all.

"I will not admit that I did something I did not do," she answered, her voice as cold as he'd ever heard it. And was that a trace of a tear he saw in her eyes? He couldn't tell; it was gone so quickly.

He grimaced at her stubbornness but nodded his head. "Four-fifths isn't going to leave you much."

She stepped away from him, looking anywhere but at him, mostly at the ground. "I'm used to not living on much."

"What happened—Nathan spent it all in the first few months?"

Claire ignored his attempts to bait her. "I want to negotiate a set time after which we will divorce."

"No."

She went over to the phone that was resting on the table in the living room, picking up the receiver and holding it out to him. "Then I suggest that you call the police and report me as a thief."

His scowl deepened to epic proportions. He didn't want to put a timeframe on his marriage, for crying out loud. So, he said the first amount of time that popped into his mind. "Twenty years." By then, they'd have at least a couple of kids, have built some kind of life together, he assumed, and she wouldn't really want to leave him after that point, anyway.

It was his best bet.

She scoffed. "In twenty years, my salary alone will have paid you off twice."

"Good. That'll take care of the interest."

She glared up at him.

"Ten, then," he offered reluctantly.

"Really? You want to tie yourself to a woman you believe to be a lying, cheating thief for that long?" Her held tilted a bit to the side as if she was surprised to hear him admit that.

That muscle in his jaw jumped angrily. "I believe in the sanctity of marriage. I don't want to get divorced at all," he countered, hands on his hips.

"Then don't marry me. You can just fuck me instead. I've already agreed to—wait! What are you doing? Stop! Put me down!"

Claire found herself lifted off the ground then bent unceremoniously over the knee he had raised by putting his booted foot on the lower rung of the nearest dining room chair. At least he didn't tug her skirt up, not that it gave her much in the way of protection. His damned hand was too hard—just like his head—for that!

"I do not want to hear that kind of language coming from you. There is a child in this household."

"I know that!" she shot back nastily, only to regret it immediately when he began to both speed up the tempo of the swats and increase their ferocity. "Ow, ow, ow! Stop that this minute! Ethan! Stop!"

"Not until I believe you've learned your lesson," he responded quietly.

"I know my lesson; I'm a grade school teacher! I don't swear!"

That got him to stop when she would have said nothing would have.

"Did you or did you not just say 'fuck' in my house?"

"But just for emphasis—and accuracy!"

The spanking resumed immediately. "We don't use language like that around here, even just for emphasis." He ignored her jibe about the accuracy of the word as it would pertain to what they would do together.

"Oh! Ow! All right, all right! I'm sorry!"

"Sorry is nowhere near good enough, as you will soon find out."

And it wasn't. It didn't matter what she said, he continued to spank her until she hung limply over his leg. And yet she had still not shed one single tear, and he had been watching—and listening—for them.

After the last swat fell, she wrestled herself away from him to stand across the room, looking wounded and indignant as she fixed her hair and clothes agitatedly.

Again, he wasn't going to be able to soothe her, and he definitely felt the lack, although he did his best to eschew those feelings. But he would bet his life that if he could just take her into his arms after he'd blistered her behind, she'd break down in tears and confess everything to him. Not that it would let her off the hook. The offer he'd just made her was a onetime deal—take it or leave it.

He'd just like to prove his theory right, and he couldn't think that confessing to him would make her feel anything but better. But he remained where he was for the moment. They needed to get things hammered out.

Ethan grimaced to himself that he had to negotiate aspects of his marriage to a woman who really didn't want to marry him. But he wanted her, and at this moment, that was the only thing that mattered to him.

"So. Ten years."

"Two."

"Eight."

"Five. And that's my final offer."

He'd been leaning against the table, arms folded across his chest, legs crossed in front of him, but he stood at that. She looked warier than he wanted her to as he approached her, although he supposed that was kind of stupid of him. He'd just spanked her. Of course, she was going to be a bit skittish around him. "Oh, but again, I have to remind you that you're really not in a place to make statements like that." He walked over to her, and he could see that she was struggling mightily to stay put as he advanced on her.

"And all of this is contingent on me being happy with you—especially in bed, but out of it, also—so I suggest that you drop the attitude."

She couldn't help but roll her eyes at him, but he could see the amount of strain she was under. It was taking a visible toll on her already.

"So, should we go to bed right now? When did you say your dad and James would be back?"

He was absolutely amazed at her suggestion, but then, he was still thinking of her as that innocent young woman who had left with another man. She'd been married for several years and was no longer a timid virgin.

Still, as much as he desperately wanted her beneath him, Ethan couldn't quite agree to that. He had a child to think about now, and he wanted everything to be above board for his sake. He didn't want there being anyone tittering behind their hands or him being teased at school because things hadn't happened properly between his father and the woman who was—or had been—his teacher.

"Five is all right," he agreed suddenly. He'd just have to make sure that he got her pregnant as often as possible, which would make it very hard for her to leave him. He knew every judge in that county and beyond, and he doubted she would want to leave their kids just to get away from him.

She looked surprised, but his diversionary tactic worked. She didn't mention anything more about them going to bed this evening, and he couldn't imagine that she was likely to ever bring it up again, considering the fact that she didn't want to do it in the first place.

He headed to his study to grab a legal pad and pen, then he began jotting down the points they had both made.

"One more thing, please."

He was the wary looking one this time.

"I don't know how or when or if this will ever happen, since I wasn't a part of it, and therefore, there's no paper trail that includes a person who knew nothing about what was going on. But if I should ever be able to produce any kind of evidence that proves that I knew nothing about what Nathan had done, everything—including the marriage—is null and void."

Ethan had to laugh at that. "Yeah. And pigs'll fly any day now."

"Just make sure that it gets into the agreement."

He surprised her by reaching out to turn her head so that she had to look at him. "You will say 'obey' as a part of our marriage ceremony, and I expect you to do just exactly that. Barring anything going on with your job, you will make yourself available to me at any time I might want you."

She shrugged, agreeing in a dismissive tone, "Of course. Isn't that the essence of marriage anyway?"

"I wouldn't know; I haven't been married. You have. Did Nathan require that you be at his beck and call?"

Her face closed up as if he'd just thrown ice water into it. "I will not discuss my marriage with you. Not now, not ever."

Ethan eyed her considerately, chafing a bit because he had a lot of questions about that aspect of her life, none of which had anything to do with his money. But he supposed she had a right to keep that information private. "Fair enough."

She pressed her hand to her forehead. "Oh, there's one more thing."

He clenched his teeth. "What, now?"

"Well, I'm assuming that I'm moving in with you?"

"Yes, of course."

"I signed a lease that lasts through the end of the school year, and I don't want my landlord to end up losing that money. She's an old widow, and my rent is her income."

It really wasn't much to ask, and he was actually impressed that she was asking it, although it meant that he was going to spend just that much more money on her, which she hated. And she couldn't imagine that he would be much of a fan of that, either.

Overall, she intended to cost him as little as possible. She was going to be the econo-wife. No shopping sprees for her. She was going to pay him back and get the hell out of here.

"I think that can be arranged."

"Thank you."

They both stood there in silence for an uncomfortable moment.

"Are we done?"

"Not quite yet," he said, gathering her into his arms to kiss the breath out of her, until she could barely take a breath of her own and ended up mindlessly clinging to him. At least until she realized that was what she was doing, stiffening immediately and trying to crane her body away from that all too intimate touch of his.

"Ah-ah-ahh, Miss Jalbert. I'm not going to tolerate you shying away from my touch when we're married, you know."

"Yes, well, we're not married at the moment." She noticed that he'd used her maiden name to refer to her rather than Nathan's name, and she wasn't surprised. If she was going to have his name shortly, then he wouldn't want to be reminded that she had been someone else's.

He let her go, and she took several large—for her—steps away from him, rubbing her hands up and down her arms in a self-soothing motion that gave him a momentary twinge, knowing she wouldn't welcome him doing that for her.

"Are we done here?" she had the audacity to ask, already heading for the door. "I have papers to correct."

As much as he didn't want to give her the impression that she could dictate to him, the truth was that he had a lot of things that he needed to get done, too. It was a rare day when both James and his father were gone, and there were a lot of things he could accomplish while they were out of the house. So, without another word, he grabbed his keys and they headed out to his car.

Even though he loved cars, and had several, the one he used around her was nothing to brag about. He wasn't about to waste his pretty MG or new Lincoln Capri on her, although he knew she'd look sensational in either of those vehicles. Cars were probably his only indulgence, and even then, he was careful not to overspend.

Instead, he brought her back to the utilitarian Packard that was the ranch's car, not that she seemed to notice in the least.

She'd never seemed to notice and certainly never acknowledged his wealth in any way, and she hadn't then, either, when he was merely a part of one of the richest families in town. But he'd made sure that the ranch diversified enough to be prosperous no matter what happened with the economy, and his efforts had definitely born fruit. They were now awfully close to being the richest family in the state, and that was saying something.

When he arrived at her sad little place, Ethan walked her to her door.

"You don't have to do that," she'd said immediately when he came around to open her door.

"I know, but if we're going to end up married, it might not be such a bad thing to let people see us together beforehand."

She nodded her head back and forth without saying anything.

He didn't press to come in and stood at the bottom of the stairs while she opened the door to her place. "I'll call you and let you know when the paperwork is ready to be signed. I've already run this by Cary, and he thinks it'll only take him a couple of days. I was figuring on us doing all of this next Friday—signing everything and then getting married."

"M-married? So soon?"

She was hardly the eager, blushing bride.

"Yes. Cary's a JOP, so he can do it for us once we've signed the paperwork. Might as well begin earning your keep, Miss Jalbert."

With that, he left, and she went into her apartment to collapse on her bed.

The essays and math tests were going to have to wait for her to finish her nervous breakdown. Hopefully, that would clear up by Sunday, so she could spend a day doing actual work, as long as she didn't think about the fact that she was going to be a married woman again—of sorts—by the end of the week.

But for now, she took a long, languid bubble bath, hoping to relax herself, although it didn't help in the least. So, she put the television on, but CBS was the only network she could get without adding tin foil to the rabbit ears and spending long moments adjusting them and praying a lot, and there wasn't anything on that she was interested in anyway.

Programming ended at eleven, and she was still wide awake. It was going to be a long night, and it ended up being an even longer long weekend.

Chapter 4

AND EVEN WITH the insomnia she was battling making every night seem never ending, Friday still came much too soon.

Ethan had called her on Wednesday to confirm that he would pick her up after school got out at three-thirty on Friday, but other than that, she hadn't heard from him since the last time she'd seen him.

Claire supposed it was too much to hope that this meant he'd changed his mind, but even she couldn't really hope for that, because where would that leave her? She didn't look at all good in stripes, and she had a feeling that he was right about just how long she wouldn't last if she actually ended up there.

Innocent people weren't supposed to be convicted, but she wasn't that naïve. They were sent to jail all the time, and she knew that she didn't want to end up there. Even putting up with him was preferable to that, she supposed, despite her bravado on occasion in front of him.

When she came out of the red brick building on the corner of Melrose and Lincoln Ave, he was there waiting for her. She suddenly felt under dressed when he approached her wearing a truly gorgeous suit that looked as if it had been made for him.

And it probably had. Someone his size could hardly buy off the rack.

She, on the other hand, had just worn one of her "work" dresses. It was nothing special, although it was clean and more genteelly worn than some of them. The idea of dressing up for her wedding hadn't even occurred to her, which wouldn't have been a good thing if this had been a real marriage.

She was one of the first out, so everyone behind her got to see him handing her a small bouquet of red roses, and she could hear all of the murmuring that was going on as the other teachers passed by her. Gloria poked her gently in the back and gave her a knowing smile when she turned around.

"Have a good time, you two," several people said, assuming he was taking her on a date.

Someone even said, "Wow! She really knows how to keep a secret!" and she had a hard time not smiling at that.

It was all a bit much, but she supposed he was right when he'd said that people should see them together, rather than them just showing up married one day. Everyone was going to think she was pregnant anyway because of the haste, but laying some ground work wasn't a bad idea.

His arm looped around her waist as if they walked together like that all the time. Claire felt very uncomfortable with the pretense, but she tolerated it until they got to the car.

His lawyer was in the city, which was about forty-five minutes away. Ethan had brought the Lincoln Capri. It was a two-door convertible, in a snazzy maroon color, with a new option called air conditioning, and wonderfully soft leather seats. Claire felt so comfortable that—against her better judgment—she very nearly fell asleep.

"Wake up, sleepyhead. We're here."

He'd known that she was falling asleep, and he'd let her do it. Ethan didn't intend that they would get much sleep tonight, so she might as well get it when she could.

His lawyer was a sweetheart—very warm and solicitous of her. Too bad she couldn't marry *him*, instead! She was surprised by how quickly the signing went. She couldn't find anything that he needed to revise, and neither could Ethan.

After that, Cary buzzed for his secretary, who came in with another woman, and then she found herself as the bride in the middle of a wedding ceremony that meant she was going to end up married to a man she didn't even much like anymore!

But there she was, listening to him intoning his vows in that deep baritone of his, and then it was time for her to say hers. She tried to keep her voice level and quiet, but she tripped over the word "obey", which had him raising his eyebrows at her. As she blushed furiously, she managed to recover and got through it.

He surprised her by producing both an engagement and a wedding ring that magically both seemed to fit her—or perhaps be just the slightest bit loose. She didn't have one for him, but she also knew that, working on the ranch, it was best that he didn't wear one anyway.

Cary produced a bottle of champagne, everyone signed the marriage license, and within less than an hour, she had become Mrs. Ferguson, and her new husband was escorting her out to their—no, his—car.

He bundled her into the passenger's side then got behind the wheel. "I can't take time away from the ranch at the moment, so we'll do a honeymoon later in the year, when things slow down."

Claire hadn't expected to have any kind of honeymoon, nor did she particularly want to have one, so that was news to her.

"You don't need to do that."

"Do what?" He looked genuinely confused.

"A honeymoon. It isn't as if this is a *real* marriage, and I don't want you spending money on me. If you're going to do that, then I'd rather you put it toward paying down my debt."

The rest of the ride home was conducted in utter silence.

But he didn't abandon his manners when they got there, handing her out of the car and slipping his arm around her waist as if he thought she was going to bolt if he didn't.

She wouldn't have, though. A bargain was a bargain. She would stay here until the debt was paid, the five-year limit was reached, or she died. She wasn't sure which one of those she was rooting for. She supposed whichever one was the shortest.

As soon as he opened the door, her senses were assailed by some incredibly tantalizing smells.

"I sent Dad and James off again—this time into the city for the weekend, so that we could have some privacy."

"Thank you."

"Our cook, Mrs. Bridges, insisted on making us a wedding meal. That's what you smell."

"Oh."

He helped her off with her coat, noting that it was really too lightweight for this time of year and not missing the fact that it was patched—quite expertly—at the elbows and that the hem was frayed. "I'll send someone from the ranch to your place to clean it out," he said almost absently as he hung it on the hall tree for her.

"Mrs. Harrington will get paid?"

Ethan crossed to the bar at the back of the living room and poured himself a scotch. "Can I get you something?"

"No, thank you," she answered politely, as if he was a bartender instead of her husband.

"You should have a sip of something. You're so stiff, you look as if you're about to break in half."

"Sorry," she murmured, taking the drink that he offered when he crossed the room to her.

"And, yes, Mrs. Harrington will get her money tomorrow, when the boys get your stuff. I'm surprised that you're so keen to see to that."

"Thank you for reminding me of what a horrible person you think I am. She's a little old lady with no money. I can sympathize with that. Just add it to my total."

"You're hardly a little old lady."

One of her eyebrows rose. "No, but she's poor, and so am I."

"So you and Nathan went through all of my money? I've wondered why your clothes were being held together by duct tape."

As soon as the words were out of his mouth, he wished he hadn't said them. She closed up tighter than the bark on a tree and turned away from him for a long moment before turning back. "Nathan was the accountant in the family. I didn't have anything to do with our money."

His "ah" dropped with doubt. Ethan raised his glass to her. "To restitution."

She had to chuff at the audacity of him expecting her to toast to that. "I don't think I'll drink to that." Instead, she raised her glass and looked him straight in the eye. "To my eventual vindication."

He gave her a quizzical look, but they both drank.

It was hardly the entwined arm, drinking out of each other's glass, romantic gestures that most newlyweds might indulge in, but then, they were hardly the average newlyweds, either.

"Hungry?"

"Yes, please."

It was a literal feast. Claire didn't think that she'd ever seen so much food in one place. It was just the two of them, but his cook had made enough to feed a family of five for a month! There were steaks and garlic mashed potatoes, cilantro rice and fajitas with all of the fixin's, lobster chowder, and several different types of salads.

She had filled her plate, but for some reason, she barely got through any of it. She hadn't been this nervous in years, and it was playing hell with her stomach.

And of course, he noticed.

"Not as hungry as you thought you were?" he asked, his voice surprisingly soft and not at all sarcastic.

"No, I'm not. I'm sorry to waste the food."

That was quite nice of her to think of, he had to admit. He did hate waste of any kind.

"It's all right. I'll save your plate. You might feel hungrier later."

He, apparently, was suffering no such attack of nerves. She didn't think she'd ever seen anyone consume so much food at one sitting. But then, he was three times her size.

Not knowing where else to go, Claire remained there with him while he ate.

As if he sensed her nervousness, Ethan kept up a running dialogue about the ranch and his father and James. She didn't say much, although she did throw in the occasional, "Oh?" and she nodded her head in all of the appropriate places, she hoped.

But she was too wound up to enjoy anything, dreading the point at which he was going to insist that they go to bed.

When they were done, she rose to do clean up, surprised to see him joining in.

"Just for the record," he said, expertly bringing in a stack of their plates while she washed the dishes, "I didn't marry you so that you could cook or clean for me. Special occasions are one thing. But Mrs. Johnson takes care of all of that for us."

A "special occasion". Was that what this was, she wondered? It certainly didn't feel like one to her.

"I don't mind," she volunteered. At least it would be something to do.

"I do," he replied pointedly.

"Okay."

Still, they got the cleanup taken care of really easily. They worked well together, which was a surprise to them both.

When he turned out the light in the kitchen, she steeled herself for him carrying her off down the hall to what she assumed was his room.

But that didn't happen. Instead, he corralled her into the living room, put on some soft, smooth music, and sat down with her on the couch after refreshing his own drink, but only filling hers about halfway and adding water to it, in consideration of the fact that she had very little on her stomach, and he didn't want to end up having their lovemaking interrupted.

Relaxed was fine. Asleep or upchucking was not.

He continued the same patter he'd kept up at the dinner table, and between the booze and the soothing tone of voice he'd adopted, she shouldn't have been as tense as she was. But it was only getting worse, the longer he delayed the inevitable.

Finally, Claire actually interrupted him, turning toward

him to blurt out in a horribly uncouth manner, "So, are we going to get this over with, or what?"

Ethan's gaze pinned hers. "Just exactly what every bridegroom wants to hear from his loving, eager bride on the occasion of their wedding night," he commented sarcastically.

She'd felt horrid as soon as she heard the words anywhere but in her head, and she wanted to apologize—she supposed—but he was already standing.

"And, yes, we can get this over with right now," he answered tightly.

Her much smaller hand was swallowed up by his, and she was being forced to jog-trot along behind him as he force-marched them down the hall.

He stopped abruptly at the door at the end of the hallway, and she very nearly crashed into the back of him, which she didn't think she would have survived. It would have been like running into a brick wall, even at so slow a pace.

Ethan opened the door to reach in and turned off the light, pushing the door open further and using his hold on her hand to pull her in.

She had to admit she was amazed by the sight that greeted her eyes. There was soft music playing from somewhere, and the entire room was alight with candles.

Claire opened her mouth to say, "It's beautiful," but before she could, she found herself spun around and lifted up against him, one hard arm around her back and the other literally ripping her dress apart from collar to hem with one yank.

As the flimsy, threadbare fabric fell to the floor, leaving her in just her panties, hose, garter, and bra, she reached for it reflexively, but he caught her cheek in his hand and held her still for his kiss.

She wanted to hate it, but she couldn't. All of those desires that had lain dormant in her since she'd left him were still right there, having been barely below the surface since she'd returned, and he was able to coax them out of hiding so easily, with just a kiss. Claire tried to hold back, tried to restrain herself, to retain some kind of control.

But Ethan wasn't about to allow her to do that. And he apparently recalled entirely too much about what she liked for her to fight him. Not that she didn't try, but it only made him chuckle.

"I remember that you used to like to fight me, to make me subdue you. I suppose I should punish you for that, considering that you shouldn't even be thinking of fighting me. But I like it when you struggle as you are. It's going to make your surrender just that much sweeter to me."

His voice had always been very potent to her, and he had known how to use it to soothe or rile her, depending on what response he wanted to elicit from her, so she was predisposed to be very tuned in to what he was saying.

But this time, it worked *for* her and *against* him. She was able to latch onto what he was saying—how he enjoyed it when she tried to get away from him, and especially that last bit about how he was going to enjoy making her surrender to him.

She employed the trick she'd used to avoid crying while he spanked her and was able to relax in his arms by focusing herself on a point that wasn't really anywhere near them, which guided her mind away from what he was doing to her.

Ethan felt the difference in her immediately, and he didn't like it one bit. She'd gone limp in his arms, like a dishrag. He had to look into her eyes to make sure that she hadn't fainted.

But she hadn't. She was simply hanging there, as if he

was the only thing keeping her from becoming a puddle on the floor.

That didn't sit well with him at all. He didn't get angry very often—he didn't often need to. His size alone convinced most people to see his side of things. But this… this was unacceptable.

He didn't marry her so that he could have a rag doll in his bed, and he intended to do whatever he needed to do to get a rise out of her. And he had a very good idea what exactly that might be.

He laid her down on his big bed—one that he'd had custom made to accommodate his size—with surprising care. But she remained exactly where he had put her, staring up at the ceiling.

Watching her as he undressed, Ethan called to mind all the things he could do to her, now that she was his. But none of that would mean anything if she just lay there unresponsive. He wanted to hear her scream his name as she came. He wanted to exhaust her with pleasure. He wanted to hear her catch her breath when he entered her, and perhaps even try to get away from his sheer size, not that he'd let her.

She wasn't a virgin, so maybe she wouldn't do that, although he couldn't imagine that Nathan had anything on him in the endowment department. The man was a ninety-eight-pound weakling, pasty and thin and bookish. Even if he hadn't been gifted with his build, Ethan would still have had to develop muscles in order to accomplish what he did every day on the ranch. He spent more of his time behind a desk than he wanted to lately. The older he got, it seemed the less time he spent riding out with the men. But he still consciously kept his hand in, for just that reason. He didn't want to end up looking like her first husband. The thought of that weasly bookworm having her first was another thought that only added to his building anger.

She hadn't moved a muscle the entire time he was divesting himself of his clothes. And when he was naked, Ethan reached down and wrapped his big, thick finger around a delicate ankle, using his grip to pull her down the bed until her bottom was at the edge of it. Then he kept hold of that ankle and grabbed the other one, holding them well apart as he stepped between the legs he was holding aloft, pressing an erection that was so hard and so painful that he felt as if he was a teenager again—and, to his dismay, with a correspondingly slim amount of control over himself. He had to be inside her, now.

Claire hadn't so much as batted an eyelash at what he was doing to her, but he thought he would probably make a bit of an impression as he nudged himself against her entrance and began to press himself into her.

At first, Ethan wanted to crow, because, regardless of whether or not she was going to participate in this—mentally—physically, her body welcomed his invasion as her dew gushed around him, easing his way. That knowledge—that at least one part of her was on his side—was all he needed to surge forward, forcing himself all the way into her with one tremendous stroke.

Her scream signaled the end of her ability to ignore what he was doing to her, and he was happy for that. But not for what he'd discovered about her that had caused her to scream like that.

She was—she had been, more correctly—fully intact.

Virginal.

Untouched.

Unsullied.

At least until now, when he could feel her trying to get away from him, to alleviate what had to be the unfamiliar pain and pressure of his undeniable presence within her.

But he couldn't allow it. He was too far gone himself to

do anything about it, although he certainly intended to get the story from her about how she had managed to remain a virgin while being married to a man for over four years.

At the moment, though, he was barely holding onto his control by the skin of his teeth, and he was losing badly to the desire—the absolute necessity—of moving.

Claire was trying to twist and slither and writhe out from under him, her hands pushing against his chest in her efforts, and he realized that it was the only time she'd touched him of her own accord since she'd gotten back—if he didn't count when she'd slapped him, and he didn't.

More for fear of her hurting herself than anything else, he rocked his considerable weight forward, onto her, which immediately neutralized her ability to get away—indeed, to move much at all. Then he gathered her wrists in one of his hands and brought them above her head, rendering her attempts to stop him from doing so embarrassingly futile.

"No, please."

He barely heard her whisper as she continued to tug against his hold on her hands. But there was no way he could stop.

When, at last, he reached the end of his ability to ignore the primal dictates of his body and he began to move on her and within her, she started to whimper and moan in the most pitiful of ways—in a manner he would never have associated with her, never have attributed to her if he hadn't heard it himself.

It was all he could do to marshal some portion of his mind away from the more feral tendencies that were quickly overcoming him over to murmur, "Shh-shh-shhh," to her, knowing that it wasn't anywhere near enough, considering what he was doing to her at the moment.

The only thing he could think of that he could do that would make this more bearable for her—besides disengage, which simply wasn't going to happen—was to do what she'd asked him about originally. Get it over with.

So, that was what Ethan did. He was embarrassed about how short a time it took him to groan uncontrollably into her ear and lose himself for that all too brief, blissful moment. But then he remembered that the embarrassment was all on him, because she apparently wouldn't know one way or the other whether he'd come quickly or taken an inordinately long amount of time.

This was all new to her. It shouldn't have been, but it was.

And still, even though his intent was to be quick about it, it had felt so good, so monumentally amazing to him, that he took much longer than he should have—in order to consider himself courteous—to raise himself up and off her.

Ethan forced himself to pay attention to her as soon as he did, expecting that she was going to try to scramble to the top of the bed or run into the bathroom and lock the door or even just run out into the night to get away from him.

But she didn't—and what she did do was much worse.

She simply lay there, not moving, not trying to cover herself—not even in the age old virginal way of innocent women—her head turned away from him. She wasn't panting or crying or reaching for her crotch—all things he would have understood if she'd done.

Every bit of him wanted to hold her, but first he wanted to clean her—the both of them—he corrected, looking down at his cock and seeing that it was smeared with a small amount of blood.

Not knowing whether she could even hear him or not, he nonetheless commanded, "Stay still. Don't move," before heading into the bathroom that was attached to his bedroom. There, he ran warm water onto a wash cloth, bringing it and a hand towel back with him, barely able to believe it when he saw that she was right where he'd left her.

Without a second's hesitation, he sank to his knees in front of the end of the bed, and gently pressing the warm wet cloth to lips that looked swollen and puffy. There was a slight trickle of blood—mixed with remnants of the both of them—that he wiped away as gently as he could. He got her as clean as he could possibly manage, not wanting her to become upset at the sight of her own blood. And then he mentally smacked himself for that thought, since she dealt with her own blood on a monthly basis.

Still, this was unexpected blood that had resulted from an unforeseen—and highly unfortunate—situation.

When she was as close to pristine as he could get her without hurting her, he saw to himself, then threw the cloth and towel in the general direction of the hamper that resided in the corner of the room before stretching out on the bed himself and reaching down to slide her slowly up to lay her head on a pillow next to where he turned on his side toward her.

She hadn't moved—hadn't made so much as a peep—while he was tending to her, and as he gathered her against him, Claire remained mute, still facing away from him.

Although she was utterly unresponsive, Ethan seized the moment to do what he'd been wanting to do since she'd returned—soothe her. He kept her locked against him, finally giving up the idea that she would look at him, and spooning her while wrapping his arms around her tightly.

He knew his erection was already poking against her behind—and she was right there, it kept whispering to him, mere inches away—but he willed himself to ignore it in favor of seeing to her.

There would be time enough for explanations tomorrow—and he was damned well going to get them. But for now, he simply held her, rocking them just slightly back and forth, rubbing her arms, and sometimes petting her hair in a way that he hoped she might find reassuring. Not that he was sure she was even really able to notice what he was doing.

She'd gone away from him—far away, he reckoned—and he'd let her stay there for a while, for the night, probably.

But tomorrow morning, he was going to want answers, and she was going to give them to him, whether she wanted to or not, frankly.

Chapter 5

ETHAN WASN'T AT ALL sure what woke him, especially since he was used to sleeping alone and her absence should hardly have disturbed him, but his eyes came wide open in the middle of the night and his first thought was to reach for her.

But what his hand came in contact with was a lot of nothing—a cold sheeted, empty side of the bed, which indicated that she had been gone for some while.

He sat up immediately, flinging the covers back and shouldering into his robe then barreling out of the bedroom, wondering if she'd taken it into her pretty head to flee out into the night, which was definitely not advisable, considering just how isolated they were here. Not that he could really blame her, considering what had happened between them only a few hours before.

Flipping lights on as he passed them, he headed for the front door, rifling through a drawer of the small étagère in the entryway that held what he sought—a flashlight. The outside light would only go so far.

As he opened the front door, he was stopped by the

sound of her voice coming from behind him. "Is there a problem?"

His drill sergeant would have been overjoyed at his perfect about face. There she was, curled up in the corner of the couch not fifty feet from him, bathed in soft lamplight and with a book on her lap.

Ethan didn't want to admit to himself just how upset he had been at the idea that she had left him like that. This was not a place for anyone to go out alone in the middle of the night, especially not a small, delicate female such as herself. Anything at all could have happened to her, and his heart had been in his throat at the thought of her walking alone down one of the few dark, dirt roads nearby.

"Who told you that you could get out of bed?" he growled, reversing his steps to turn out all of the lights he'd just turned on.

One delicately sculpted eyebrow rose at that. "I wasn't aware that I had to ask permission—"

"Well, now you know," he interrupted curtly.

She gave him a little frown, and he wasn't sure whether it was because he'd interrupted her or because he'd given her a rule she wasn't too keen on. But she continued with her explanation nonetheless, "I've been getting out of bed on my own since I was about five. I have insomnia, and I didn't want to turn the light on in the bedroom and risk waking you. I have weekends off, but I remember from knowing you previously that ranchers don't get much time off."

He appreciated her concern but detested the tone of voice she was using, although there was technically nothing at all objectionable about it. It was calm and even and soft. And entirely devoid of any kind of feeling—even anger.

If there was one thing he couldn't stand from her, it was indifference. He'd rather she railed at him, screamed and cried, and called him names, than to simply sit there as she was, breathing slowly and looking at him as if she was about as interested in him as she would have been a scorpion if it had appeared before her.

Not really knowing why her demeanor was annoying him so thoroughly, he stalked up to stand in front of her, putting his hand out to her in silent demand and watching—and getting even more worked up—as she put a bookmark in her book, put the book on the side table, turned off the light, unfolded herself as she stood, and—lastly, as if it was the thing she least wanted to do—put her hand in his.

His fingers closed around hers immediately, just before she found herself tugged against him then lifted into his arms and carried—bridal style—down the hall to his room, after he'd leaned down just enough to snag the bottle of scotch he'd been diligently working on emptying since he'd heard she was back in town.

He could have just slung her over his shoulder. He could have transported her there in a lot of different ways that wouldn't have been very pleasant for her, but he chose that one, which surprised her.

And even though she knew that he was angry with her—for some reason other than the fact that he thought she had stolen from him, it seemed—he didn't drop or throw her on the bed, but rather laid her gently down on it.

Claire had donned both a nightgown and a robe, and he made short work of untying the belt to the robe, separating the two front pieces as if he was unwrapping a particularly delightful present.

She just lay there, as she had done before. She wasn't even watching him, he noted. Her eyes were closed.

Well, he wasn't about to let her remain unaffected again, although he wasn't going to demand sex from her so soon after he'd taken her virginity.

When he heard the phrase in his head, he stopped. He'd

taken her virginity, not that idiot Nathan. He could hardly believe it.

That phrase reminded him of several things, and one of them sent him to the bathroom to retrieve the cup that was always there. Once back on the bed, he poured a healthy amount and took a sip then put the glass on the headboard where it would be handy.

Then he addressed the other thing that he had been reminded of. "How are you feeling?" he asked as he stretched himself out beside her.

No response—no indication that she'd heard him at all.

"Claire," he said much more sharply and with no small amount of demand.

Her eyes opened at that. "I'm sorry. Did you say something?"

He was looking impatient again, and she knew it was a direct result of her deliberate remoteness, and that was just too damned bad for him. What did he think she was going to do? Make love with him with all her heart and soul? She was giving him access to her body, like any good wife would do. He had not stipulated—nor would she ever have agreed to—any kind of requirement that she participate in her own degradation.

"I asked you how you were feeling."

"Fine, thank you," came her pat answer.

If she was trying to get under his skin, she had found the perfect way to do it, not that he could let her know that.

"I'm glad to hear that. Even here, though?" he asked, reaching boldly up beneath her gown to cup her womanhood.

She tried to hide her slight start at his unfamiliar touch, but he felt it anyway.

Even more primly, if that was possible, "Yes, thank you."

"You're not sore at all?" he probed, although not with his hand at all.

Despite what he thought of her and the embarrassment his query conjured, Claire was not in the habit of lying. "A little, I guess."

That was an understatement, but she didn't consider it a lie. He had fallen asleep very quickly once he'd hauled her up against him, wrapping his big body around hers in a way that she wanted to find smothering but, instead, found very comforting.

Still, he was snoring in her ear, and she was much too wound up from everything that had happened today to fall asleep. So, she'd gotten up and gone to the bathroom, which had proven to be a bit of a dicey endeavor—a painful endeavor, actually, which she hadn't thought to expect.

Nor had she expected that there would be blood, but she certainly knew the reason why there was. It wasn't much, and she was glad of that, because she didn't fancy wearing a sanitary napkin around him, with all of the unflattering pictures that conjured in her mind.

She wasn't really sure why she cared about that—it was going to happen at some point in the future. But she'd always hated all of the unsightly, unwieldy, and often ineffectual apparatus that it involved, and it was so cumbersome and thick—it was like wearing a diaper. She'd just gotten done with her period, so she was just as glad that she could put it off, at least for a little while.

Then she headed for the living room, made herself comfortable on the sofa with one dim light on, and dove into her book, hoping against hope that it would make her sleepy.

Ethan leaned over and grabbed the glass. "Here. Have some of this. It should help some with the pain."

It was a pretty big drink—there was a lot of scotch in there—and Claire worried that it would go to her head.

Ethan *hoped* that it would. He was betting that—especially on her empty stomach—it would relax her a bit and perhaps make it harder for her to find her way to wherever it was she'd gone to last night, while lying right next to him. Hell, while lying beneath him!

There wouldn't be any pain this time—he'd see to that—and he was going to do everything he could to make sure that she remained mentally and emotionally engaged with him the entire time.

She took a very small sip and tried to hand it back to him, but he gently pushed it back toward her. "All of it, please, peach."

She frowned, and he thought she was going to out and out refuse, which would have meant that he wouldn't be able to keep the vow he'd just made to himself that she wouldn't experience any more discomfort this evening, because then he'd have to spank her—and good, too. He wasn't about to let her think that he was going to allow her to get away with disobeying him, even in something small.

He watched her stare at the drink and pause for a moment, but then she downed it in two gulps, handing the empty glass back to him when she was done. He put it out of their way, on his nightstand.

Ethan knew that it was going to take a little bit for the alcohol to do its work, but that was fine with him. He intended to indulge himself with his new wife until then.

"Take off your robe and nightgown, please," he asked in a husky voice that was barely above a whisper, but Claire knew she couldn't refuse, regardless. "While we're alone, you may wear your robe if you're cold, but no clothes in bed, ever."

She wanted to pout at that declaration, but she forced herself not to. Instead, she quietly did as he asked, leaning down to lay the both of them at the foot of the bed, then stretching herself back out next to him, fully naked, like some kind of sacrifice.

Once she'd presented herself to him like that, he could see her doing it—going away from him in her mind. She was uncomfortable being naked in front of him. He could understand that. But he wasn't going to put up with her ignoring him. So, he set about making sure that she couldn't, with her body's full cooperation.

Ethan smiled softly—not that she could see it through her perpetually closed eyes—when he realized that her nipples were peaked. The house was cool but not cold enough for that.

He wondered at her as his eyes swept over her in limitless appreciation. Damn, he'd forgotten how gorgeous she was! Granted, he frowned a little, because she was also a damned sight too skinny! He knew he should have made sure that she ate more of their dinner, but he'd remember to make certain that she ate enough—to his standards—from this point on.

Still, even thin like this, she was everything he'd ever wanted in a woman—firm, full, pink berried breasts, delightfully curved hips, a beautifully shaped behind that just cried out to live in a state of perpetual blush, and that utterly arousing mound of hers, decorated, as it was, with a crown of soft curls.

He indulged himself by running his hand down the length of her body, noting the slight differences in skin, the feeling of her too prominent ribs beneath his fingertips, and even delighting in her knobby knees, which he'd teased her about before.

"Turn onto your tummy, please."

He was glad when she did as he asked, and he didn't have to repeat himself or rouse her from whatever reverie she disappeared into. At the moment, he was just as happy to indulge himself in what he knew he now—finally—possessed.

And she was at least as gorgeous to him from this view, too—the small shoulders, the perfect line of her back, those gorgeously generous hills—still faintly pink from being spanked last night—delicate ankles and pretty, tiny feet with their pink jellybean toes.

Again, he let his hand lay claim to all of that territory after his eyes did, rubbing her shoulder, tickling slightly down her back then squeezing a cheek before following the line of her legs to the soles of her feet, which he leaned down and kissed then nipped slightly.

That foot his teeth had just left had jerked—just barely, but enough to give him hope that she was finding it harder to dismiss him through the booze he'd given her.

"Onto your back again, please, wife."

He liked using that term with her. In fact, it gave him more pleasure than he wanted to experience, hearing it in his own voice. And he would have sworn that he saw her almost frown upon hearing it from him, as if it was a curse rather than an honorific.

She lay before him again, legs primly closed, hands at her sides.

"Put your hands above your head, please, Claire."

Her eyes sprang opened and she looked at him. He would have sworn that he saw just the slightest flash of rebellion in them—or was that fear—but then she closed them again and quickly complied with his request.

"What would you like me to do with them?" she asked, as if she was asking him to pass the salt.

"Just leave them there. If you move them below the top of your head, I will punish you."

He watched her as he said that but couldn't discern any

response in her body language or expression at his declaration.

This time, when he set his hands to exploring her, it was both of them, and they headed to the spot he was most interested in—her breasts.

As he recalled, she had inordinately sensitive breasts. At one point, years ago, when they had been petting rather heavily, he had thought that she wasn't far from orgasming as he'd played with them, but she hadn't.

And he didn't do what—at some point in the future—he was sure to. He didn't simply grab them and squeeze them roughly, tugging at the nipples without a care for whether or not he hurt her, but purely to satisfy his own needs.

No, this time he was going to make damned good and sure that she climaxed, and although he knew that a little pain might help her do that—because she seemed to enjoy more than a bit of it—he was of a mind that she was already sore elsewhere, and he didn't want to add any further discomfort. Unless, of course, she misbehaved.

But since she seemed to be so dedicated to her dutifully compliant wife/dead fish act, he doubted that that would happen. At another point, he would spank her—not because she'd displeased him or disobeyed him in any way, but again, simply for his own purposes, which he knew would likely translate into hers, too, anyway—whether or not she wanted them to.

She was more of a sensualist than she knew—or, more likely, was willing to admit—and Ethan was again amazed that Nathan had been able to keep his hands off of her. But that man's misfortune was his own considerable gain.

He kept the touch of his fingers light and teasing, only occasionally pinching the ripe tips he found there and never hard enough to hurt. Ethan endeavored not to ignore the rest of her breasts, either, cupping and squeezing them, licking every inch of them and bestowing soft kisses to their tender undersides.

He was alert to any sign of response from her, but there was none, save for the fact that she was breathing more heavily than she had been when he'd started. He'd known he was going to take his small victories where he could, so he had paid attention to those tiny indications that he was getting to her, and he savored each one of them.

Moving over her, he held himself above her, bearing his weight on his hands.

"Spread your legs wide for me, *wife*." His voice was carefully quiet but firm.

His eyes caught a definite flinch, although he wasn't sure whether he should attribute it to the order he'd given, or his emphasis on the title "wife". He didn't much like the idea of it being either, but he was glad to have gotten something out of her.

Ethan waited for a long moment, longer than he would have later in their relationship by far, but he didn't see any indication that she was moving to obey him at all.

Just as he opened his mouth to say her name in a deep, scolding tone, her thighs began to make their way in different directions.

"Good girl," he murmured deliberately, and he was sure that he heard her usually slow and steady breath catch at his praise.

They stopped, of course, long before he wanted them to, and he did have to scold her with her name. At one point, Ethan threatened to put her over his knee and was rewarded for his patient efforts by a small but very exasperated sigh before she finally complied and opened herself to him as fully as he required.

If she had obeyed him more readily, he would have praised her again, warmly. But as she had hesitated, he chided her instead. "The next time I tell you to do that, peach, I don't expect to have to help you with it, nor do I expect to have to wait for you to decide to do it. Whenever I tell you do so something, the decision has been made—by me—that you *should* do it, and your bottom will fare much better if you move as quickly as possible to obey me."

Although he didn't say this to her, overall, he was elated by her progress. He'd determined years ago that she responded really well to a combination of praise and punishment, although not in equal measures. Claire could be a strong willed and stubborn woman, and he knew that, four out of five times, she should get the stick rather than the carrot.

But the carrot was never to be put aside entirely. It was very useful, and he used to love how she would melt against him when he complimented her—always honestly—about her physical appearance or told her how well she'd done in obeying him. Her body loved the punishment, and her mind loved the praise. He knew that the judicious use of both of them was the key to keeping her on her toes and—most importantly—with him, not off in her own little world.

Maneuvering himself down the bed a bit, he cupped his hand over her gently, and even so, she started a bit before she could get herself under control.

"If you'd open your eyes, you know, you'd be able to see what I'm going to do, and you wouldn't be scared when it happened," he commented casually. He wasn't going to make it a rule that she had to keep her eyes open, but if she didn't start doing that on her own, he could see it becoming one, sooner rather than later.

She sighed at that but in no particular manner that he could discern.

"Am I hurting you, touching you like this?"

"N-no," she answered honestly.

"Good girl." He would swear she contracted at that, but he wasn't sure it wasn't just wishful thinking on his part.

His fingers moved downward a bit, toward her opening, pressing themselves in between her lips very gently. When they hovered just above her opening, he heard her hold her breath.

"Does this hurt, baby?" he asked, letting his real concern shine through to her in his tone.

She almost squirmed but checked herself. "No..." she answered.

"But I bet you are sore inside, though, hmm?"

His eyes flicked upward to see that her face was beet red.

"Claire?" he prompted, seconds later. Her embarrassment should not prevent her from answering him and would not save her from a punishment if she didn't.

"Uh, yes."

It was barely a whisper, obviously dragged out of her against her will.

"Well. Let's see if I can do something to help. I'll kiss it, and then I'll make you feel better."

Her eyes wanted to open widely at that, but Claire kept them closed. What on earth could he mean by that? How could he possibly kiss her there? *Why* would he kiss her there? Why would he *want* to kiss her there? It didn't make sense.

When Ethan had situated himself between her legs, with lots of him hanging over the end of the bed, not that he cared in the least, the first thing he did was put his fingers back where they had been.

And this time, she definitely flinched.

"Shh-shh-shh," he soothed. "I'm going to touch you a little bit, but I'm going to do my best not to hurt you. But I want you to lie still, Claire."

He waited for her to agreed or say something, but she didn't.

"I need you to acknowledge what I've told you to do. I'm never quite sure whether or not you're hearing me."

"Yes."

Two big fingers parted her lips again and were immediately drenched. He had a hard time not shouting in triumph, but he somehow managed not to. That told him an awful lot about how well he was doing in handling her. It seemed that he had found the right way to coax her out and keep her with him—he hoped. Oh, he was certain that the alcohol had helped a lot, and he didn't intend to have to get his wife drunk every time he wanted to make love to her.

But he intended to wage a campaign of keeping her well and thoroughly punished, but tamping that down, taking the edge off it with carefully controlled and crafted doses of pleasure, such that she wouldn't *want* to hide herself away from him. And, eventually, he hoped, she wouldn't be *able* to. It might take some time, but he was quite sure he'd be successful, as long as he was patient and consistent.

Ethan crooked and twisted and crossed his fingers, dampening them in the overt evidence of her desire until they were very thoroughly drenched. Then he brushed them up, through those beautiful lips to a clit that looked terribly swollen and uncomfortable.

In fact, she whimpered—however undetectable it might have been if he hadn't been paying such close attention to her—when his fingers found her, and that was almost enough to bring him off right then and there. His hips actually bucked against the mattress on their own, as if he was driving himself into her instead of barely touching her.

Keeping his fingers together, and using only the gentlest of pressures, he began to worry her clit with them, brushing back and forth over it very quickly, not stopping, not letting up at all.

Claire was finding it impossible to keep still like she

wanted to. She didn't want to give him the satisfaction of showing any kind of response to what he did to her. But this was unavoidable! It felt so good, she thought she was going to faint. She couldn't control her panting, and seconds later, her hands began to grab for something—anything—solid to hold onto, but the only thing she found was the headboard, and that wasn't what she wanted.

Something was happening to her that was utterly and completely out of her control, and she didn't like it, not one bit. She'd rather that he would do to her what he'd done last night a thousand times—despite the pain—than do this once. It was awful and wonderful and wonderfully awful.

And then, as he continued to molest her in that terribly embarrassing manner, she felt her façade of withdrawal and detachment slipping away as some strange, compelling, and overwhelming pleasure took its place. She had to do something!

So, she opened to say what she'd wanted to say since he'd brought her to his bed, setting aside her pledge of neutrality, not even caring in the least if she sounded as if she was begging him—because she was! "Stop, please! I can't! I can't stand it!"

To her enormous surprise, he did exactly that.

But what he ended up doing was much, much worse. "I'm sorry," he apologized, "I haven't even done what I said I was going to do, have I? I said I was going to kiss it and make you feel better."

With that, he leaned forward and pressed a kiss to her injured part—well, the outside, anyway. At some point, he'd press his tongue inside her, but he thought that would be a little much for her at the moment. So instead, since he'd kissed her, he set about making her feel better.

Claire could barely deal with the idea of his mouth being on her *down there*, and then, suddenly, he did something that was even more unexpected. He sealed his mouth—his *entire mouth*—over that overly sensitive spot on her that he'd been teasing with his fingers and began not only to suckle gently at it but, also, to lap the tip of his tongue over it.

And over it.

And over it.

She had no idea what to do with all of the pleasure he was inflicting on her. She had nowhere to put it, no way to cope with it.

"*No! Stop! Don't! Pleeasse!*"

Then it settled there, his tongue, right on that spot as it pressed itself against her, moving very slowly up and down and back and forth and every possible way, directly on top of a place that she was sure was going to drive her crazy. That was when her hands came down to land on those broad shoulders of his as she tried frantically to push him away from her.

But the second her hands touched him, she found herself flipped over quite expertly. One of his arms settled across the small of her back, and the hand at the end of the other was beating out a terribly painful rhythm on her rear end!

And, having let go so far in regards to the pleasure he had been bringing her, she was then completely unable to reclaim her former detachment when faced with the searing pain of him branding her fair skin with his palm unrelentingly. So, there was little else Claire could do other than succumb completely to the urge to scream and beg him to stop, while utterly exhausting herself in a futile attempt to getting away.

Now this was more like what he expected from her, Ethan thought as swat after swat landed on that beautiful bottom of hers, until it quickly became a dramatically bright red from the top of her bottom to the top of her thighs.

This wasn't a long, drawn out punishment, though. He

deliberately kept it short and sharp and hard—and hard to deal with—not giving her enough time to come to grips with it before he'd flipped her over again and placed himself right back where he had been, with his eager mouth latched tightly onto a clit that had increased quite considerably in size, even in so short a time.

And even though—or perhaps because—he had been tanning her hide.

This time, Claire arched into his mouth, rather than away from it, although she kept up a steady stream, much like a chant or a prayer, that beseeched him to stop, until he lifted his mouth from her just long enough to scold her lightly but firmly, "Shh. Quiet now. Close your mouth, unless it's to moan or scream. The pleasure you feel now is nothing compared to what it's going to be, I promise. And it's going to happen. I don't want to hear you beg me not to again. There's nothing to be afraid of. You couldn't be in a safer place than my arms, and in a moment, you won't want to be anywhere else."

Then he was there again—where she least wanted him to be but surely would die if he wasn't. Something wild and uncontrollable was building within her, and despite what he'd said to her, she couldn't help but be a little bit afraid of it. More than a little bit, truth be told.

And when the inevitable happened, because he refused to stop, and he felt her entire body begin to slowly stiffen as she arched herself into him again while keening and moaning and finally screaming out loud with it, she lost herself much more completely than she did when she removed herself from him.

It was nuclear. It was the alpha and the omega. It was the secret to life. It was a raw and primitive paradise, an inherently primal bliss—and every single second of it was utterly, totally, and completely out of her control. She did lose herself—to him.

And she hated it with the same white hot passion that she knew—instinctively—would make her crave what he could do for her for the rest of her life.

But it did accomplish for her what she'd been trying to do the entire time, too, although she didn't have the slightest bit of control about that, either. She checked out from the situation more completely than she had ever been able to in her life.

Once those unbelievably blissful contractions had died down considerably, she realized that he—her husband, Ethan—how strange that thought felt or might feel if she could feel anything at all at the moment—was busy moving things around. She thought he got up at some point and moved the covers around, tucking her under them. She noted that some of these things were happening around her, but she didn't feel any connection to them.

Until, all of a sudden, as he began to move her under the covers, she did feel. All of it. All at once, that wild tumult of emotions flooded into her mind, and it was too much. Much, much too much.

Everything she'd been avoiding feeling descended on her like the hounds of hell, and she could tell that she was going to lose it more totally than she had in a very long time—since she'd cried herself into being sick, months after she'd married Nathan, when she'd realized what a big mistake she'd made.

As he was placing her under the sheet from one side of the bed, she was slipping out the other side and heading—hell bent for leather—to the bathroom.

And, she found as she closed the door behind her, there was a lock on it!

It was entirely too loud a lock—she thought the

neighbors could probably hear her engage it—but she did so anyway, knowing it wasn't going to make him very happy. But she was beyond worrying about what he thought at this stage. Then, as the tears roiled behind her eyes, she made a quick decision, turning the water in the vanity on full stream, and then she did the same with the shower.

And that was all she could do before the storm swept her away. Claire hunkered down in the corner of the big shower stall. She could hear him beating on the door and calling her name, but, surprisingly, she'd had the presence of mind to look, and there was no key to the lock.

So, unless he wanted to break it down, which she didn't necessarily put past him, but she still doubted he'd do it, she was relatively safe from him. That lasted about three minutes.

She was still well out of it, though, when she felt his arms wrap around her, lifting her away from the water, which had turned cold by now. She was too far gone to even wonder how he'd gotten in. She hadn't heard any wood breaking, but she couldn't be sure she'd have noticed it, even if it did.

As she stood shivering, he toweled her off, keeping her close to him and his natural furnace-like heat as possible while he did it. When he'd gotten her as dry as he could, Ethan brought her back to the bedroom, pulled her nightgown over her head—after just having told her that she wouldn't be able to wear one in bed with him—then tucked her under the covers, spooning her from behind like he had last night.

She was still shivering and sniffling a little, but she wasn't actively crying. He wasn't sure if she'd stopped because she'd cried enough—although he doubted it—or if it was because of her proximity to him, which he thought was probably the real reason.

She'd not cried much before, either, but he had seen her

cry. She wasn't one of those women who refused to do so on principle, thinking that it made her look weak. She just wasn't anywhere near as predisposed to it, and she didn't use tears as a weapon at all, as some women would.

It had worried him, though, that with all of the radical changes she was going through, and Lord knew she'd been spanked enough, she hadn't cried *at all*, that he knew of. He supposed she could have been doing that when she was in her apartment alone, but he hoped that wasn't the case.

He was here now, though, and he'd never shied away from a crying woman in his life. He'd had a sister that he'd adored, and he'd held her often enough—and learned from her—that sometimes a woman had to cry. He accepted—and expected—that his wife would, too.

He'd almost gotten another small pour of whiskey to have her take before she fell asleep, but he decided against it. If he'd judged things correctly, she'd had a massive orgasm, and then a massive crying jag. He was pretty sure that just one of those was pretty well guaranteed to help her sleep.

Both of them meant that she might well sleep all night. He'd been sorry to hear that she was still suffering from insomnia, and he was determined to help her with that in any way he could. Except for the catharsis she was experiencing, he had a good idea that intense orgasms just before sleep might be a big help in that area.

For her part, while he was thinking about how glad he was that he was there with her, Claire wasn't at all used to making such a spectacle of herself, and in general, she preferred to cry alone. Nathan had understood that. She corrected that thought with ruthless honesty. Nathan didn't care to be bothered with her when she cried, so she did it alone in the bathroom.

She desperately wished she was alone, and since she'd been stripped bare of all of the walls she'd built up for her own protection, she couldn't stop herself from saying hoarsely, "I want to go sleep in one of the other bedrooms."

It was an enormous house, and she knew that he kept other rooms ready and waiting for guests.

"No," he answered flatly, with no trace of sarcasm or any kind of edge.

She swiped her hand over her nose as she sniffled, whispering, "Please."

Ethan's arms contracted around her, holding her very securely against him—not because he thought she'd get away from him, but because he knew that some women found that soothing.

The way he was holding her was his answer, and he didn't bother to give her another verbal one. And it turned out that he was right.

She was asleep—breathing slowly and steadily—within just a few minutes, but he continued to hold her for long into the night after that, checking on her occasionally, tucking the covers in around her, and keeping watch over her.

It wasn't even a choice—on his part—to do that.

It was just something he had to do.

More than that, it was something he *wanted* to do.

Chapter 6

IT WAS the Monday morning after they had gotten married, and things were a little frantic as both she and her new nephew were getting ready to go to school.

Ethan usually drove James in, and he insisted on doing so for her, too, even though she had her own car.

That put Claire out a bit—not that she let him know it, though—because she was used to coming and going whenever she wanted to, and she liked to arrive at school early, have a cup of coffee, and slide into her teaching persona. But she wasn't going to be able to do that today, for no particular reason she could fathom, other than that's what her husband wanted.

As she sat down in her chair—gingerly, at best—she wondered if she was even going to be able to do this for the next five years. Or the next five minutes.

Mrs. Bridges set an enormous amount of food out on the dining room table, and both Halloran, Ethan's father, and James dug in as if they'd never tasted food before. She saw Ethan reach for his own plate, too, but then he appropriated hers, instead, putting a good-sized scoop of scrambled eggs, a homemade apple cinnamon muffin, and some fruit on it.

And he didn't have to say anything when he put it on the table in front of her. He just caught her eye, and she knew what he expected her to do. That was one of the reasons she was sitting so tenderly this morning—one of the many reasons.

Her husband had decided, in his infinite wisdom, that she needed to gain weight. She had told him that the last time she'd gone to a doctor—which, she'd admitted upon his closer questioning, was several years ago—he had told her that she was the perfect weight.

"Have you lost any since then?" he'd asked.

Her face had clouded over at that. "I don't know," she answered stubbornly, although it was the truth.

"Well, I think you need to eat some more. You're skin and bones."

She didn't volunteer that it was partly because she and Nathan had had no money—especially toward the end when she wasn't working much because she had to take care of him, or that she didn't have much money now because she'd barely begun to get a paycheck, since they only paid monthly, and with moving expenses, she couldn't afford to buy much food.

So, even just in the short time they'd been together, he'd taken to making a plate up for her, which, if they had been on better terms, she might have found endearing. And she knew that he tried to take her small capacity into consideration, but still, he gave her much more food than she could eat several times over the weekend. And he'd caught her throwing it away.

So, she gotten spanked immediately—bent over a chair in the dining room—bare assed as he swatted her viciously with a wooden spoon that she resolved she was going to put in the barrel where Hal burned trash as soon as she thought she could do so without getting caught. That thing was horrid, and she was going to make damned good and sure that its life expectancy was mere days. Hours, even, if she could find a time to do it, along with anything else she could find in the kitchen that might be used against her by him.

How could something so small feel so God awfully stingy?

It was worse than it might have been, though, because she'd committed two cardinal sins, as far as Ethan was concerned. She'd wasted food, and she'd disobeyed him.

She would have gotten a somewhat lesser spanking if she had simply told him it was too much. He would have judged whether she had eaten enough, then told her to put what she didn't want into a bowl and put it into the refrigerator.

Claire had deliberately waited until he was in the shower—she thought—before she attempted to throw the food away, too.

He'd caught her in the act and had delivered her spanking while he was as buck naked as she was. She'd never understand how he could be so casual about nudity. He'd decreed that, when they were alone, he didn't want her to wear anything, and she was having a terrible time with that rule.

She was inordinately grateful to Hal and James when they got home. She was so glad to have someone else around, because it meant that she could keep her clothes on! She'd spent the entire weekend with absolutely no protection from him, of any sort at all! She was naked, and all he had to do was lift her onto that ever-present spike he sported twenty-four hours a day, seven days a week around her, apparently, and hurl her into an ecstatic oblivion at will, it seemed!

And when he decided she needed to be punished, there

was absolutely no delay, no need to take down or unbutton or unzip anything. It was absolutely horrid.

The spankings and the sex were incredibly hard to adapt to, especially when she was still trying to detach herself from both of those experiences, and he was having a truly alarming and disconcerting amount of success at not letting her do that—already! What was it going to be like for her in a couple of years? Hell, at that pace, a couple months? All he'd have to do is look at her and she'd orgasm right then and there in front of him or anyone else, by that point, she was quite sure!

But what was almost worse, in her opinion, was when he was really nice to her. She much preferred Ethan the Demanding Ass to Ethan the Caring Husband, as he'd been when he'd first subjected her to the incredible pleasure to be had from sex.

And there were other things he did, like being worried about her weight, or tenderly seeing to her after he'd made her lose her ever loving mind in ecstasy, or when he'd coaxed her into dancing with him, holding her gently against him and Texas two-stepping to the sounds of Hank Williams, while the both of them were—as usual—completely nude. Those all made it harder for her to hate him as much as she knew she should. She tried to remember that she was here against her will, to pay off a debt for a crime she hadn't had anything to do with, but her flesh was weak—*very* weak—and would beg to differ about that.

He was also unfailingly solicitous to her, always asking her how she was and how she was feeling, and even disgustingly polite, too, always giving her orders, but couching them with a terribly civilized "please" or "thank you"—even during a punishment or in the middle of sex.

She really didn't think she could deal with this. It wasn't turning out to be at all what she had expected. It was much worse and much better but in entirely different ways from what she had anticipated. And, what was worse than all the rest, was that she had the horrifying feeling the same loving emotions she'd had toward him when they had been together previously were beginning to seep into her brain, despite how horrid he had been and was continuing to be to her.

With that unhappy thought, she rose to go into the bedroom, heading toward the bathroom to give her hair and make-up one last check before they left.

It was ridiculous how just going to the bathroom now was a reminder to her of just how committed he was to keeping her close to him as she entered the room without needing to open the door.

He'd removed it that night when she'd locked him out, and he'd informed her that he didn't intend to replace it any time soon. So, for the first weekend of their marriage, it had simply leaned up against the wall next to the gaping entrance to the bathroom, and he had only grudgingly put the door itself away when she'd pointed out that it was likely to prompt people to ask some embarrassing questions.

"I won't be embarrassed in the least to tell them why it's there," he'd replied blithely.

She'd just given him a resigned sigh at that and turned away, heading for anywhere he wasn't.

To her pleasant surprise, the next time she'd entered the room, it was gone, although she would have been much happier if he'd just put it back, even if he removed the lock. But he wasn't giving her that option, and she had already vowed—and broken it so many times she couldn't count—that she would ask for as little as possible from him.

It was bad enough that he seemed to be insisting that they play the part of a loving couple. James was out the door as soon as the car rolled to a stop, with a wave and a "Bye!"

as he ran toward his friends, who were getting off the bus he usually took.

She tried to do much the same thing but heard him utter one word and stopped, just as her hand found the door handle. "Stay."

So, he got out and came around to open her door, but that wasn't all he did. He insisted on escorting her into her room, which, of course, had everyone around them tittering and gasping. He even came inside, with everyone following him, and then he publically declared that they had gotten married that previous Friday, and that she was now Mrs. Ferguson.

Everyone clapped and said congratulations, then oohed when he took a small present out of his suit coat, saying, "For you, my beautiful bride."

It was a replacement for the name plate she kept on her desk, and it read, of course, "Mrs. Ferguson". Just seeing it was a bit of a shock to her. She definitely hadn't come to grips with the reality that that was her name now, for however long.

They both graciously—Claire a little less so because she was feeling so lost—accepted everyone's congratulations, and he finally left, but not before he kissed her very lovingly, which got everyone "awing" at him again.

"You certainly caught the best one of the bunch!" all the other teachers were telling her as they crowded around her.

Gloria chimed in, "And you never once let on as we were all drooling over him at Margret's just days ago!"

"That was awfully quick," was generally agreed on.

"Well," Claire said, a bit defensively, "we were dating before I married Nathan."

That seemed to be an excuse that everyone would buy for how quickly they had gotten married, although she knew that—if she got pregnant—they'd all still be counting the months to the day she gave birth.

She hoped it would all die down from there, but then he had to pick her up, of course, and he arrived in her classroom with a big box of chocolates and another, bigger bouquet of roses.

"You two should have a reception. No one got to go to your wedding, but we'd all love to celebrate with you."

"I don't think so," Claire began.

But then Ethan picked up on it as he held her tightly to his side with a possessive arm around her waist. "Well, we hadn't thought about that, but we might well have to do it. We could throw a bit of a shindig at the ranch, couldn't we, honey?"

"If you say so, dear," she answered meekly but with a patently false smile as she looked up at him that he recognized, but she doubted anyone else did.

Claire really hoped that was all she was going to hear about in regards to a celebration about their wedding, and indeed it was, for a couple of months.

But the idea had stuck in Ethan's craw, it seemed, because he brought it up again, at a time when she was just starting to get settled into her new role—not just as wife to him, which was more than demanding enough, but she was also now a de facto mother to James and a daughter-in-law to Hal.

Even with Mrs. Bridges' help, she felt overwhelmed every single day, even though Hal was wonderful. He was everything she could want in a father-in-law, especially since he seemed to always take her side against his son, which only endeared him to her just that much more.

The first time she'd gotten in Dutch with him in front of Hal, he had sent her to their room as if she was a child to wait for him. She heard muffled voices and knew that he and his father were having words, too, but that didn't make her feel any better.

And the fact that James was already in bed only one room away and Hal was probably still in the living room hadn't deterred him in the least from giving her a very sound spanking that she came very close to howling about while over his lap.

So much for remaining unaffected by his efforts—sexual or otherwise. She was already well on the way to losing that battle entirely, and she had been from the first time he'd touched her.

He'd taken her afterward, too, as he had gotten into the habit of doing and which she didn't like at all. It was damned hard to remain mad at him when he everything else he did to her seemed designed to either bring her to the heights of pleasure or treat her like spun glass.

She even loved it when he pressed himself into her, once it had stopped hurting. And he'd been annoyingly wonderful and patient about making sure that he didn't fuck her before she was fully recovered, either.

But, boy, once she was, he took her at least once every night and usually in the morning, too. And although she rarely got any sleep weekend nights, he exhausted her so completely that she often slept very late in the morning, and she knew that he did his best to make sure James was occupied outside of the house, so that he wouldn't disturb her.

She'd been surprised to find that Hal was up one night when she'd not fallen asleep in his arms as she now usually did, and she'd been surprised to see him when she'd wandered out into the living room to read her book and wonder exactly what it is that she was doing with her life.

"Oh. I'm sorry. I don't mean to disturb you," she said,

attempting to duck back down the hall, even though she had no interest in going back to bed.

"You're not disturbing me in the least, Claire. Come and sit with me. I'd love to talk with you, if you'd like, but it's fine if we don't, too."

She made her way to the place she usually occupied in the living room. She'd created a bit of a nest in that corner of the couch, so she headed there.

"Couldn't sleep?" he asked.

"No."

"Ethan mentioned that you have insomnia sometimes. My wife suffered from that, too. I wonder if it's more of a woman's ailment."

"I don't know. Could be," she answered.

"Do you mind talking, or would you rather I kept my big trap shut?"

Claire had to smile. "I'm fine to talk if you'd like."

"Well, as you can imagine, your marriage was a surprise to us all."

"Yes."

"But I wanted to tell you that I'm very glad you're here. I'd kind of given up on the idea that that big oaf of a son of mine would ever get married, especially after you left town with Nathan."

Claire had the grace to color at that, but she really didn't know what to say, so she kept quiet.

"I don't know if he told you or not—I suspect he didn't—but he loved you then. He'd gotten my mother's rings from me—her engagement and wedding rings—and had them sized for you. He was going to pop the question the next time he saw you."

Claire was stunned—completely stunned. She'd had no idea then, and she certainly had none now. That's why the rings she was wearing had fit her so well. He already had them from before!

"I take it, he didn't tell you?" Hal garnered from the dumbfounded look on her face.

"No. He didn't."

"Well, he can be stubborn and willful and opinionated—"

"And bullying and domineering and pushy," she added, and then they both chuckled.

"Yeah, that's him, all right. But I do believe that he does love you, even now. When you left, he was like a wounded bull. He beat up anyone who looked at him sideways, drank too much, and was a complete bastard to everyone around him.

"But then Melanie and her husband died, and James came to live with us, and he had to straighten up and fly right, which he did, although I know it wasn't easy for him. He might go off the deep end sometimes—as everyone does—but overall, I think Ethan generally tries to do the right thing."

She might have to argue that point, but she didn't. His father didn't need to know their business, and she wasn't out to taint his view of his son.

"And when you came back, he reverted a little."

A lot, she thought.

"And you haven't been here very long, but you've already been good for him. You give him someone else to look after, and a man like Ethan needs someone to care for, to work for—otherwise, why is he working himself into the ground? You're helping him with that, whether or not you know it. He works fewer hours already, just so he can be with you. That's a good thing. You're getting him to enjoy himself more. Another good thing. And when you give him children, he'll have even more people to love and take care of. More good things."

She shook her head slowly. "I don't think he loves me, Hal."

Hal shook a finger at her. "Don't you believe that. He'll tell you in his own good time."

Claire hesitated. "There are things you don't know."

"I'm sure there are, my dear," he agreed, rising slowly and with a low, pained groan. "And I haven't asked you whether you love him, because there are things I shouldn't know. I just wanted to make sure that you realized—whatever else is going on between the two of you—you're good for him. I hope—but I have my doubts—that he's as good for you, too. Perhaps that, too, will come in time, if my sometimes bastard of a son opens his eyes and realizes what he has in you. I know he's sometimes hard on you, but believe me when I tell you that it does come from a place of deep emotion, of love."

He kissed her on the cheek and took her hand, saying, "Welcome to the family, Claire," before tottering off to his own room.

She thought she'd get away without having to wear a fake happy smile during a wedding "celebration" that she didn't want to have, but Ethan was quite keen on it, and he wasn't going to let her convince him otherwise.

"But there's no need of it."

Claire could see that muscle jumping in his jaw and knew that she was close to pushing him too far.

"I want us to have a party to celebrate our wedding. Everyone—except the bride, apparently—wants to come to a party to celebrate our wedding. Thus, we're going to have a party to celebrate our blasted wedding!"

He wasn't yelling, but he might as well have been.

And she was just about as angry as he was about it, although she wasn't quite sure why, except that she objected to the sham of it all. It was bad enough when he insisted on playing her loving husband in public. His reputation with her coworkers as a wonderful, loving, attentive husband was sealed forever in their minds, and that had now extended to most of the rest of the town, since he'd insisted that she accompany him almost everywhere he went, despite her obvious reluctance.

She was terribly afraid that she was softening toward him. Her anger at the situation she found herself in was much harder to access than it should have been.

And she was terribly afraid that she was falling in love with him, when that was the last thing she wanted to do. He already had too much power over her happiness as it was. If she fell for him, that would be the last straw. There'd be nothing left of her to fight him with. She'd stop caring whether she was ever proven innocent of the crime he was sure she had committed, whether he ever realized just how wrong he'd been about her.

It wasn't a conscious decision to do so on her part, but Claire felt as if, at that moment of true despair and hopelessness, an impenetrable, protective curtain had been drawn around her, and she became almost unnaturally calm. The detachment she had cultivated in order to deal with the intimacies she was forced to endure—and which were crumbling into dust due to his efforts in that area—had come to roost in the other areas of her life, in which he had less overt control.

"All right," she agreed, turning over and away from him. If he wanted her, he would take her. There was nothing she could do to stop him or to curb her own desires for him. But she didn't have to feel anything else that she didn't want to.

Ethan watched her turn over and sighed. He didn't really understand why she had such a problem with this. Yes, their marriage wasn't quite the same as everyone else's, but didn't most women like parties and gatherings and get-togethers? Wasn't that what most of them spent their time doing, especially when they didn't have a job to go to?

Who didn't like good food, good friends, presents, and cake? He'd explained to her that he didn't want some kind of starchy thing with suits and ties and ball gowns. He just wanted to invite the townspeople—that they'd both grown up with—to their ranch for a good time. Mrs. Bridges and a couple of hired people would do all the work, really. It wasn't as if he was asking her to cook and clean and bake everything herself.

He was of a mind to want to turn her over and talk to her about it some more, but he let it go. But over the course of the next few months, while the party was being planned, almost entirely without his wife's input, Ethan began to watch her even more closely than he usually did.

Sometimes, more often than not lately, Claire worried him.

Yes, he had found the secret—relatively quickly, for which he was eternally grateful—to not letting her check out in her mind and lie there beneath him as if it was happening to someone else. Once he pushed her past that point, as he did each and every time, she was something to see. In the midst of her passion, she was utterly wild, and he'd come to crave seeing her like that—utterly uncontrolled—as often as he could.

He thought he had found that delicate balance he'd wanted to achieve with her between pleasure and pain, keeping her nearly fully revved but tempering it with frequent spankings. The time between when she did her best to ignore what he was doing to the time that she began to writhe and moan in his arms was getting shorter and shorter each time he pulled her into his embrace. And he could not possibly get enough of her. If Dad and James hadn't been here, he would have dwelt inside her on a nearly permanent basis.

But he'd seen that she was really just as withdrawn, just as disengaged from him—from almost everyone—as she had been when he'd first taken her to bed. She was unnaturally quiet, her usually buoyant personality dampened dramatically. She rarely smiled or laughed, speaking only when spoken to. She did everything she should do, went where she should go, and functioned in a way that was utterly normal. But not for her.

There were two areas where that dramatic change was not true: her work and James. James was a shining light. He was bathed in her good humor, he received all of her smiles, and it went without saying all of her hugs. She didn't spoil him but still showered him with attention, spending long hours playing with and reading to him.

She very obviously loves his James, and she told him so frequently. Whenever he came into the room, she brightened visibly and smiled. She never looked at him like that.

And now, here he was, at the low point of his life, being jealous of his nephew. Ethan dragged his hands over his face as he lay there, facing his wife. He'd exhausted her again this evening, forcing her to orgasm after orgasm using his lips and fingers and cock, until she begged him to stop, and even then, he brought her to two more, just because he wanted to.

She was asleep now, though, facing away from him. He could hear her even breathing.

He'd never been able to deduce what she had against their upcoming gathering. He just knew that she was dreading it as if it was a firing squad rather than a party. She'd not contributed anything to its planning that she hadn't been asked to do—not one idea about decorating, music, food, nothing. He and Mrs. Bridges and even Dad had done it all themselves.

Even his dad had helped more than she had. That said something troubling right there.

The only contribution she'd made to the discussion about the party was that she wanted the invitations to say "no presents", which he had, of course, accommodated.

How she was behaving was indicative of the fact that he hadn't been able to break the code of her indifference outside their bedroom—and that was something he hadn't liked at all, either.

It was a small thing, but it bothered him, and he quickly forbade her from doing it. She had been calling the ranch "his" house, their bedroom "his" room, "his" cars, etcetera. He'd corrected her several times, spanking her for it and emphasizing that he didn't see things that way at all—that everything was "theirs".

Claire hadn't argued about it, but sometimes, she still slipped, and it annoyed him more than it should have when she did. Perhaps because he knew she didn't believe that he thought that way, and he knew that stemmed from their agreement and how he had maneuvered her into his life and his bed.

That damned agreement was more of a pain in his ass than anything else, and he already wished it didn't exist, but he supposed it was a reality of their situation. He didn't have a doubt that she'd be long gone without it, and he had no one to blame about that other than himself.

Sure, fifty thousand was a lot of money, but the truth was that he'd gotten along without it even then, and he—they—were more than well off enough without it now. Someday, he hoped to tear it up or burn it in front of her. All of the money he was getting from her salary was just accumulating in a bank account that he'd set up for her, anyway.

She was, understandably, very hung up about money, and she did her best not to cost him anything extra, to the point of being annoying about it. He was careful with his money, but he liked to enjoy its use, too, though. Claire didn't want him taking her out to dinner or to the movies, and she'd tried to decline new clothes, too, until he'd laid down the law about that, right on her pert backside, especially when she'd told him to put them on her tab, much like she'd made that smart remark to him about their honeymoon.

Unable to stop himself, he reached out and carefully brought her into his arms, having already learned how to do so without waking her. He slept best when he knew right where she was, even though holding her like this made his chest ache.

He didn't like to see her miserable at all, though, as much as he'd thought that was what he would want when he first envisioned all of this. That was just leftover anger at the loss of the money, but much more so, the fact that she'd left him for Nathan.

Ethan held her close all night, and by the time the sun crept over the window sill, he was out of bed and out on the range, riding hard and exhausting himself after having made the hardest decision of his life.

Chapter 7

"CONGRATULATIONS and best of luck to the both of you!" Cary Davison pronounced at the end of his sweet toast, holding his glass of champagne aloft before drinking a sip then shaking Ethan's hand and kissing Claire's cheek.

If they'd had a normal wedding, he would have been Ethan's best man, so he had demanded to be able to make a toast to them, and it was very loving and heartfelt.

Hal had already had his turn, and Gloria had wanted to go next. But Mrs. Bridges tapped Claire on the arm and she turned toward her, as far away as her husband's steel band of an arm would allow.

"I'm so sorry to interrupt you during the party, Mrs. Ferguson, but there's someone here to see you."

Claire looked confused. "Someone who wasn't invited to the party, I take it?"

"Yes."

"Well, who is it?"

The older woman wrung her hands on the skirt of her apron. "He says his name is Beaumont, Mr. Troy Beaumont."

Claire sagged heavily against her husband for just a second then straightened immediately, but Ethan was much too attuned to his wife not to have noticed that she had very nearly collapsed.

"What is it, darling?" He turned toward Mrs. Bridges, too.

"It seems we have a visitor," Claire stated, still staring at the cook and feeling dazed. "It's my husband's—my previous husband's—brother, I believe."

What she'd said stunned him so completely, too, that when she tried to step away from him, he let her.

Ethan had the presence of mind, though, to turn back to their guests long enough to say, "Carry on without us. We have an unexpected visitor, but we'll be right back. Eat, drink, and be merry while we're gone!"

Then he fairly sprinted after his wife. He wasn't about to let her meet him alone.

Mrs. Bridges had had the presence of mind to show him into Ethan's study, thankfully, and when they entered, he turned and Claire could definitely see his resemblance to Nathan.

"Claire? Claire Beaumont?" he asked, walking toward her with his hand out.

"Claire Ferguson," Ethan corrected, stepping up behind her and putting his arm around her waist.

"Of course," he agreed. "I'm Troy Beaumont, Nathan's brother. It's very nice to meet you finally."

He shook Claire's hand.

"Mr. Beaumont, this is my new husband, Ethan Ferguson."

"Your housekeeper told me that you'd gotten remarried. Congratulations."

"Thank you. Won't you please sit down?"

She and Ethan, who was stuck to her like glue, sat on one

couch on one side of the room, while Troy took the other.

"As I said, I'm sorry we didn't meet before, but I take it that you and Nathan didn't have a very big wedding."

"No, it was just us and the JOP."

Ethan frowned at that. She'd never talked to him about her marriage to Nathan. Not that he really wanted to hear about it anyway, but he had no idea that she'd never had a "real" wedding.

"He and I used to correspond quite a bit. I live out in Oregon."

"I remember. You have a farm of some sort?"

"An orchard, actually. Pears, mostly, some apples."

"I bet it's beautiful out there," Claire complimented.

"Oh, it is, it is. You should come see it sometime. I'd be glad to have you—and your husband, of course."

Ethan had heard about enough chitchat. "So, what brings you all the way here, Mr. Beaumont?"

Claire frowned, and she might have elbowed Ethan, but she checked the impulse.

"Well, I have to admit that I took much longer getting here than I intended. I meant to find you shortly after Nathan passed away, Mrs. Beau—"

She thought she heard Ethan growl, and Mr. Beaumont got the hint.

"Mrs. Ferguson, but I had some financial difficulties. But I'm here now, and I apologize for the delay."

"That's no problem, I'm sure," she reassured the man.

"Well, I came because I received a letter and a package from Nathan not long before he died, and I found the contents of both to be quite disturbing. But Nathan charged me with finding you once he'd passed, so here I am." He dug a letter out of his pocket and produced a small, square package. "I was just going to mail it to you, when I realized that you'd moved back to Somerset. But considering its contents, I didn't have enough faith that it would arrive to you in tact, so I accompanied it."

Then he handed the letter to Claire.

"Read it, please. It'll explain why I'm here better than I can."

She opened it and began to read.

"Out loud, please," Ethan commanded, somewhat impatiently.

Dear Troy, I hope this letter finds you in better fettle than I am. The bare truth of the matter is that I don't believe I have very long to live, and I wanted to confess to someone what I've done. I know you will be shocked to read this, but I trust that you will come to forgive your ne'er do well younger brother, as you always have in the past. You know that I had a job at Ferguson's, as a junior accountant. But what you don't know is that I was taking money—always in small, discreet amounts—from the Ferguson Ranch accounts for quite some time, and it has added up to a tidy sum—somewhere around fifty thousand dollars, give or take.

You also know that I had been dating Claire Talbert for some time, and that we left Somerset and got married some time ago. I've used some of the money for our living expenses since then, but quickly came to regret my rash act, and we have stopped using those ill-gotten funds altogether, despite the fact that, with my infirmities which require that Jane tend to me constantly, that leaves us quite destitute.

"Still, I no longer want to be associated with the funds but can't quite bring myself to turn myself in, especially when death is so near. At least I will have Claire in the end. She has been a wonderful wife—much better than I deserved—and she is totally innocent of my crime. I never discussed my—our—finances with her. She knew absolutely nothing about what I had done and only ever profited from it in any way when I spent money from it myself.

The package contains the remains of the funds, which is only a few hundred dollars short of all of it. I'm sending it to you because I know that you will know what to do with it. Bless you, Troy. You have been a wonderful older brother. Forgive me for my sins. Yours forever in Christ, Nathan.

At that, Troy opened the package, so they could see that it contained an enormous amount of money, and handed it to Claire.

"It's not my money, Mrs. Ferguson. I think it's yours to do with as you please. I don't want to have anything to do with it. I just wanted to make sure that it got to you."

Stunned beyond belief, Claire still managed to say, "Thank you, Mr. Beaumont, for all of your efforts in this matter, for coming all of this way. I would never have known, one way or the other, if you had just kept it. You are obviously a man of great honor and integrity."

Then she turned and handed it to her husband, saying with truly sickening sweetness, "I believe that this is yours, dearest."

Ethan was floored by what had just happened, and he accepted the money from her automatically, looking down at it and then up at her, then down at it again before he straightened and turned to the other man in the room, who was gathering up his things to leave.

"Mr. Beaumont, do I take it to understand that you have experienced some financial problems, which caused you to delay getting the money to us?"

"You," Claire said under her breath. "The money goes to you. It's yours, not ours."

Ethan ignored her.

Mr. Beaumont answered the big man nervously, in a rambling sentence that he couldn't seem to stop, "Yes, sir. My wife died, and my little girl is seriously ill. My sons—I have three and they're all good boys but young yet—have had to work the land without me, which means we've taken in a lot less than we need."

"Mr. Beaumont, I am not trying to accuse you of anything in any way."

Must be nice, Claire thought to herself.

"I asked that question merely to clarify what you'd said before about your finances. And my wife was quite right. What you've done here—taking money out of your own pocket when you could ill afford it—to bring this to us is a truly an act worthy of a reward." He offered the box full of money to Mr. Beaumont. "And in that vein, I would like you to have this."

Mr. Beaumont looked as if he was going to faint. "But, Mr. Ferguson, I couldn't possibly."

"Of course, you could. Use the money as you need it. Get your daughter to a doctor. Hire some hands to work the land. Buy more land. Buy a better house. Send your children to good schools. I know by the selfless act you have just performed that you will put the money to good use." He clapped the astounded man on the shoulder and shook his hand. "Thank you for everything you have done here today, Mr. Beaumont. You will never know the totality of it. Thank you. If you don't mind, I'll send Mrs. Bridges to show you out."

He wound up his conversation with the other man rather abruptly because his wife was making her way toward the door without him, and Ethan wasn't at all sure that she wouldn't simply continue out the front door and out of his life after this!

He caught up to her and held the door open for her, but she didn't head anywhere but back to the party, to his great surprise and incredible relief, but he couldn't seem to shake the feeling that she was destined to bolt out of the house at any moment.

She was more involved than she had been before the arrival of her previous brother-in-law. She actually smiled at people, attended to James' unending questions with her usual loving patience, and when they cut the five-tiered cake that Mrs. Bridges had so lovingly crafted and fed each other a piece, she didn't smash it into his face as he might have thought she would.

Instead, she took a finger full of frosting and painted a stripe down the line of his nose, pressing an extra dollop right at the end, all while smiling so brightly that his heart caught.

He couldn't lose her. He couldn't. Ethan knew that she had every right to scream and yell and rail against him, and, yes, to walk right out the door and never have anything to do with him again. He couldn't believe that she was still here, and he couldn't keep himself from constantly touching her, keeping her even closer to him than he usually did.

"You two newlyweds!" everyone said whenever he'd dip down and kiss her lips or her cheek or pull her to him for a hug.

She didn't even seem to be avoiding his touch as she surreptitiously had—as much as he would allow her to anyway.

Claire didn't eat much. She had a mouthful of the cake, and he had brought her a plate of delicious goodies he thought she might like, but she had picked at it at best.

Unable to stop himself, he caught her to him at one point, pressing his mouth to her ear. "You've had a reasonable amount of champagne, baby. You need to have something more to eat, please."

She leaned back and caught his eyes. "Or what?"

"What do you mean, 'or what'?"

Claire looked up at him and stated quietly, "I know you were just in that room with me. And I know that you know that there's a stipulation in our agreement that, if I was ever proven innocent, then you, my dear husband, are null and void."

With that—and ignoring the terrible growl coming from behind her—she turned away from the bear she'd just poked mightily and walked over to where the ladies from school had all drifted together, as they would.

As soon as she sat down, Judy Trumbull nearly swooned. "Oh, my word, your husband is such an incredibly good looking man!"

"Yeah," Margaret agreed. "And unlike a lot of really good looking men, he only has eyes for you."

"Why, he's staring at you right now, I believe!" Terri informed her.

But it was Gloria who gave her what she wanted. "Here. It's a sin that this is your party, and you don't have a drink in your hand. Have a margarita."

It was the first one she'd ever had, and it was wonderful! It tasted like angry lemonade, and she downed it very quickly then reached for another one.

"Slow down, cowgirl! Those are full strength, and I'm not sure you should have another."

"Stop being sush a spoil sport, Gloria," Claire pouted, turning to find her husband, who was indeed staring right at her. She raised her glass to him then took two enormous gulps. "I'm celebrating."

But before she could get to the third mouthful, she felt herself being lifted, and suddenly Ethan was right there. He smoothly relieved her of her glass, put a plate full of food down on the table, then picked her up and sat down with her perched on his knee. "I think you've had more than enough of this, peach. How about if you have something to eat to absorb some of that alcohol, please."

Again, all of the women around the table "awed" at how well he took care of her.

Ethan smiled at them all. "I hope you don't mind a rooster in the hen house."

"Of course not!" they all chorused at him, and Claire rolled her eyes as she tried to remove the hard arm that was around her waist.

His mouth found her ear again when he whispered firmly, "Stop."

He'd trained her too well, even in so short a time, and she did.

Rather than forcing her to eat anything, Ethan chatted amiably with the women while breaking off pieces of a big, frosted brownie that was just right chewy. Some of them, he ate himself, others, he put on a plate for her. And they did disappear. Next, he took apart a cinnamon roll, and so on, carefully giving her much more of the treats than he ate, and by the time he allowed her to stand to go to the bathroom, she was much more clear headed, although still a bit tipsy.

"If you'll excuse me, ladies," he said, following closely after her.

"They don't go to the bathroom together, do they?" he heard someone ask from behind him.

Ethan followed Claire through their house and down the hall toward their room, but she took a sudden right hand turn that surprised him, into one of the unused bedrooms.

"Where are you going, Claire?" he asked, speeding up a bit belatedly.

"None of your business anymore, Mr. Ferguson," she replied, beating him into the bathroom and locking the door behind her.

Ethan leaned against the doorjamb. "Bull. You'll always be my business. You're my wife."

"For as long as it takes me to find a good 'vorce lawyer."

That sent a chill through his body, but what could he say? Nothing was ever going to be enough.

"Claire, I-I'm—"

"Go 'way! I'm trying to pee!"

It was all he could do not to just sink to the floor, but instead, he headed out to the party to seek out Cary.

It was nearly eleven before everyone left, and the happy couple stuck around with everyone, although they weren't glued to each other's sides any longer. But the groom's eyes still followed the bride around the room as greedily and eagerly as they had before.

Claire helped Mrs. Bridges with doing some preliminary cleaning up of the mess, swallowing down as much of the extremely excellent champagne her husband had forked over while she stacked the dishes.

When she nearly dropped a load of them before she got them to the counter, the older woman gently suggested that she might want to lie down.

"Good idea," Claire agreed.

Mrs. Bridges wondered where her husband was when she really needed him. Usually, he fairly hovered around her, but right now, he was nowhere to be seen. That was mainly because he was holed up in his study with the last of that bottle of whiskey, with another one handy to replace the dead soldier.

She made her way to the bedroom she shared with her currently—and surprisingly—absentee husband only long enough to grab her nightgown, robe, slippers, and something to wear tomorrow, since she was likely to be up long before he was. Then Claire headed to the bedroom she'd been in before to pee, locking the door behind her more as a statement than because she thought it would deter him in the least.

She knew for a fact that it wouldn't, and this one had a key, so he wouldn't even need tools to get to her.

She fell face first onto the bed, literally, and waited for the sweet oblivion of all of the alcohol she had consumed this evening to overtake her and put her to sleep. Only, of course, it didn't happen that way. It couldn't possibly be that easy for her.

Instead, she lay there, wide awake, listening for his footsteps and playing everything that had happened today—especially Mr. Beaumont's visit—in her head again and again and again and again.

It was at least an hour or two later before she heard his heavy footfalls, hearing him pause in front of the door but then proceed—somewhat drunkenly, she thought—down to his own room.

She wished she was still drunk, but all of the damned food he'd packed into her over the course of the evening had sopped up the alcohol she'd consumed, so she was wide awake *and* sober, and she was going to lose her second husband in less than a year very shortly.

Claire raised an imaginary glass in the air. "To me. Widowed and divorced in record time."

It felt strange to her to be in such a small bed and to be alone. He was always such a big presence even within his equally big bed, that even though this was a normal double bed, which most couples slept in, Claire felt very alone.

She didn't want to admit that she missed his arms around her—before and after she fell asleep. He always held her wonderfully tight, usually while her body was still throbbing—in several areas at once, depending on how well behaved she had been—and she could feel his big body curled around hers. It was the safest feeling she'd ever experienced.

Just thinking of how he used to take her and tease her and make her scream for him had her gushing in her panties, and before she could think about the many reasons not to do it, Claire got up, put her robe on, and headed down the hall to his room.

The door was unlocked. He didn't have anyone he needed to keep out. She slipped in and closed the door quietly behind her, leaving her robe on the end of the bed, as was her habit. Moonlight streamed in from the windows to the left of the bed, and she could see that he was lying there—in the nude, she'd bet—with his arm over his eyes.

For a long moment, Claire indulged herself in something she had never allowed herself to do before—she just looked at him. He was a magnificent specimen—all hard and well-muscled and angular—and more than ready, too. She could hardly miss that!

Her mouth literally watered from the sight of him, and parts of her wanted to just sling a leg over him and mount him. So, she did. Just as she was bringing herself down to him, she ended up on her back with him looming over her.

"What are you doing here, Mrs. Ferguson?" he rasped drunkenly.

"Fucking Mr. Ferguson," she replied, tilting her face up to kiss him, full mouthed and full hearted, for the first time since she'd returned.

Ethan could barely believe that she was here, but he wasn't going to question his luck any too loosely. He was ready, and he'd bet that so was she, so he began to press himself inside her.

But Claire put her hand on his shoulder. "No, stop."

"What do you mean, stop?" he asked, barely able to comply with her request but trying his best anyway.

"I mean, roll onto your back and let me do the work, Ethan."

He was off her practically before she finished the sentence, and he savored the sound of his name on her lips.

But she didn't simply reconnect them. Instead, she did what he had done to her their first night together. She touched him everywhere, from the top of his head, where she ran her fingers through his hair, to the soles of his feet, where she found to her surprise that he was ticklish, and everywhere in between.

Then she began to concentrate on the less neutral areas, flicking his small nipples, biting them gently, while her hands roamed over his muscled shoulders and down his flat belly.

"Holy—God—Claire, I don't think—"

"Shh, shh, shh," she echoed him again. "You've had your fill of me. Now it's my turn."

"No," he countered huskily. "Never my fill."

She chose to ignore that in favor of dragging her mouth down the center line of his body, until it literally caught on his twitching, throbbing cock.

It was more than she could take, even now, when he'd been teaching her how to please him that way, although she was more willing now and was able to accept more of him than she had. And he was damned appreciative of her efforts if his moans and the way he was trembling were anything to go by.

The idea that she could make him shake filled her with power. Claire reached down and cupped his balls, rolling them gently and squeezing them a bit, as she knew he liked.

"Claire… Claire, if you want me to fuck you, then you can't keep doing that."

She was over him in a flash, holding him in her hand so that she could guide him into her. Even now, it was a struggle for her to take him, although her weight helped. His hands on her hips didn't give her much choice, especially when there was only an inch or two more to go, and he thrust himself up into her while holding her down for his invasion.

Claire cried out at how amazing it felt to be filled with him.

"Shhh, baby," he cautioned, not wanting James to awaken and interrupt them.

"Sorry," she breathed, beginning to move herself up and down on that enormous pole between her legs.

Long moments later, he was the one getting scolded to keep quiet, but before she got the full admonishment out, she found herself beneath him again, his shoulders holding her legs up and back, while his mouth latched onto a bobbing nipple and one hand covered her mouth as the other found her eager bud.

"I want you to scream as loudly as you can from behind my hand. I want to hear everything you're feeling as you come on my cock, Claire," Ethan demanded.

And, for the first time, when it overcame her, he heard her scream his muffled name as he buried his face in the pillow next to her and did the same for her.

Although she loved the feel of him on top of her, whether they were having sex or not, Claire tapped his shoulder, asking primly, "Would you roll off me, please?"

Ethan immediately assumed—as she'd known he would—that he was smothering her, which seemed to be a particular concern for him, although he'd never come close to doing that.

Still, his concern worked to her advantage, and as soon as he was off her, she got up, donned her nightgown and belted her robe around her.

Ethan swallowed hard. "Y-you don't have to go if you don't want to."

He saw the small smile on her lips and felt another chill. "Oh, but I do, Mr. Ferguson. I do."

The next morning, she slept much later than she usually did, and when she came out of her room, she was fully dressed.

She wandered into the kitchen. Neither Mrs. Bridges nor

the usual big spread she cooked every morning was in evidence. Unfortunately, her husband was.

He was sitting at the dining room table as if he'd been waiting there for her for some time. "Good morning. Can I get you some coffee?"

"No, thank you. I'm going to go into the bedroom, unless you're going to use it, and move some stuff out."

She saw him grimace out of the corner of her eye and had to remind herself that she no longer cared.

"Could I have a moment of your time before you do, please?" he asked.

"What for?"

"I have something to give you." Ethan pushed an envelope toward her, and she noticed another piece of paper that looked alarmingly familiar in front of him.

She was intrigued, so she took the envelope. But it was the paper in front of him that she addressed first. "Why do you have a copy of our agreement?"

"So I can do this," he said, flicking a lighter open and catching the bottom of it, so that it went up in flames in seconds, while he put it in one of the big ash trays that were kept around for Hal, who smoked.

"That's very dramatic, but it's not like I don't know that it's no longer valid."

"I know."

"And I'm free."

"I know that, too," he agreed, pushing the envelope at her again.

"What's this?"

"Open it and see."

It was a check for fifty thousand dollars.

Claire caught his eye and gave him a quizzical look.

"I'm sure you know that this was never about the money. I don't need the money. I could have used it more then, but it didn't cripple us when Nathan stole it." Ethan cleared his throat but kept his eyes on hers. "This has always been about you leaving me for Nathan and how much I wanted to make you pay for doing that. And, just plain how much I wanted you. I've never been able to get over you, to get you out of my mind."

He gestured toward the check. "That's all of the money that's gone into the account that was set up for you to pay me back—the money you earned through teaching, plus some."

"Plus a lot," Claire exclaimed. "I didn't make anywhere near this in the months we've been together."

"I know. But it's an amount that kind of cleans the slate, as much as that is possible."

Then he stood suddenly, and Claire took a step back, which stunned—and humbled—him. "I just wanted to say that I'm sorry for everything I've done to you. Most especially for not believing you in the first place about the money. I should have known that you wouldn't have anything to do with it—deep down, I'm sure I did, on some level. I just wanted you so badly that I was willing to overlook any evidence to the contrary and the fact that I know you're a better person than that. And I'm sorry that you had to live in such poverty with Nathan."

"How could you know about that? You didn't have anything to do with that."

"Still. I'm sorry for all of it." He sat down heavily in the chair, speaking to her for the first time ever while staring at the floor. "I wanted to give you an amount of money that would allow you to be independent of me, so that you could do what you want. You could travel or get your masters or live anywhere you want."

Claire could hardly believe she was saying this, but she took a step closer to him and asked, "Could I live here?"

His head shot up and his eyes locked onto hers. He was

so astonished at what she'd just asked that he stuttered, "Why, y-yes, of course, you c-could!"

"I have the rest of the school year to work out, since Sally's not coming back. And all of my stuff is already here. I was just going to move it into the spare bedroom I slept in last night."

"Oh, oh." His second "oh" was full of dejection. "Yes, that would be fine."

"I really don't want to leave," she continued, taking another step closer to him, dragging her fingertips on the mahogany table while she did so. "I've definitely grown to love Hal—"

"And he loves you, too. Hell, I think he loves you more than he loves me!"

That got him a brilliant smile. "Of course, he does, Ethan. And I love James, too."

"He is your little shadow. He worships you. You are one of the best things to come into his life, first as his teacher, and now as his aunt."

"He is a darling little man. You've done very well with him, Ethan. Really."

"Thank you, Claire." Her sincere praise made him choke up a bit and blush, which he never did.

"And I think that I could come to love another member of the family, if that member of the family was willing to be patient and give me the chance."

Ethan started to get up again, certain that the person she was talking about was him. "Of course—"

But he didn't get very far before her fingertips on his chest pressed him back into his chair, and Clair looked down at him with a mischievous glint in her eye then back up again, peering around as if looking for someone. "Now where *is* Mrs. Bridges? I need to talk to her—"

She didn't get through her teasing before he roared and

grabbed her up in his arms, settling back down with her on his lap.

"If you will stay here with me—with us—I will be as patient as you need me to be, I promise."

His wife gave him a doubtful look. "Don't make promises you can't keep, Ethan. Patience has never been one of your virtues."

He waggled his eyebrows at her obscenely. "Yes, but I have so many others of them."

"Then where have you been hiding them?" she asked innocently, and he growled.

"I know you said that you thought that you could grow to love me, but I want you to know that I already love you. I think I've loved you for a very long time, Claire."

"I know, Ethan. It's one of those few virtues you were talking about…"

The End

Carolyn Faulkner

The words "spanking" and "discipline" have always sent a shiver up Carolyn Faulkner's spine. She knows she's not alone. Writing started as a way to explore her feelings. Soon short stories flowed from her pen featuring reluctant heroes taking the leading lady in hand, but always for her own good.

Today Carolyn is the author of dozens of books. She writes from her home in Maine, where she lives with her husband and leading man.

You can read an interview with Carolyn here:
http://www.blushingbooks.com/blog/?p=175

You may check out her website while it's under construction here:
http://www.carolynfaulkner.com

Don't miss these exciting titles by Carolyn Faulkner and Blushing Books!

Series books

Military Daddies

Lieutenant Daddy
Captain Daddy
Colonel Daddy
Major Daddy

Gentle Series

Her Gentle Giant
Her Gentle Cowboy
Her Gentle Soldier
Her Gentle Gangster
My Book

The Alpha's Woman series
The Alpha's Woman
Kosh's Omega
Red's Mate
An Omega's Awakening
The Omega Within
Mate of the Omega Collection

Adored series
Adored
Tessa's Wedding

The Red Petticoat Saloon series
Grading Garnet

Thornton Brothers trilogy
AJ's Hope
Beau's Desire
Cade's Wish
Thornton Brothers, Three-Book Set

Taken as His series
Prima
Tria

Priceless Love series
Priceless
Love's Possession
Dangerous Love

Mistress Mommy Series

Alicia, Book One

Little Miss Series

His Little Miss

Little Francesca

Military Daddies

Captain Daddy

Lieutenant Daddy

Single Titles

Come to Me

The Gentleman Cowboy

Love Vs. Goliath

The Viking's Conquest

Second Chance Nanny

The Inconvenient Marriage

Promises, Promises

Love Cares Not

More Than All Right

Rescue Me

His Queen

Her King

Maddie and Daddy

Transgressions

The Brothers Rule

The Eye of the Beholder

Made to Order Bride

His Sugarbaby

Mr. Sunshine

No, Sir

His Runaway Bride

Undercover Sir

The Lark and The Bull
Doctor's Orders
A Babygirl for Christmas
Her Handyman
The Hart of the Matter
At His Hand
King of Hearts
True Desires
Lord Belden's Baggage
In His Care
Correct Me If I'm Wrong
Beauty Of The Beast
Tamed To His Hand
Daddy!
Amanda and the Stable Master
Lion
The Banished King
Northern Belle
The Cherished One
Forever Wife
Grace's Demon
Beauty's Beast
Captured by the Count
Male Order Bride
Sinful
Packed: The Enforcer
Submissive Love
A Heart Full of Heaven
Daddy's Girl
To Love a Man
Etta's Surrender
Her Secret Submission
Make Me
Let Me In

'Til Death Do Us Part
Promises Kept
The Obedient Wife
Old enough to Know Better
To Trust Her Heart
Naughty Girls: Brynn and Kim
After Hours: A Medical BDSM fantasy
Droit de Seigneur
Dutch and the Cowboy
Under the Lash
The Rogue and the Rose
Submissive Bride
The Unrequited Dom
Three's Company
All Hallow's Eve
The Reluctant Bride
His
Embraced
Attentions Throbbing
Submissive Desires
Kept
A Hard Man is Good to Find
The Spoils of War
Gilded Cage
Second Chances
Patriot Bride
The Boss of Her
Forever and Always
Tribute
Caged
The Substitute Wife
Captured by Time (w/ Alta Hensley)
A New Forever (w/ Alta Hensley)
Bound by Love: A Carolyn Faulkner Trilogy

Tears of a Vampire, and Vlad's Story, Two-Book Set
Never Say Never
Under the Cover of Love
Her Guardian Don
Her Knight In Faded Denim
Forever In Love
Depths of Desire
The Power Of Love
Only Her
On the Razor's Edge of Paradise
Indiscreet
A Most Unsuitable Mate
Make Me Yours
Ready For Love
The Gentleman Dom
The Supplicant
Belonging
Hidden Desires
Her Bad Boy
All Is Right With the World
The Error Of Her Ways
At His Hand

Holiday Stories
A Holiday to Remember
Griff's Christmas Angel
A Season to Submit

Anthologies
Tamed By The Cowboy
Blushing Cheeks Vol. 1
12 Naughty Days of Christmas2017
12 Naughty Days of Christmas 2021
Dominating His Valentine

Blushing Books

Blushing Books is one of the oldest eBook publishers on the web. We've been running websites that publish spanking and BDSM related romance and erotica since 1999, and we have been selling eBooks since 2003. We hope you'll check out our hundreds of offerings at http://www.blushingbooks.com.

Blushing Books Newsletter

Please join the Blushing Books newsletter
to receive updates & special promotional offers.
You can also join by using your mobile phone:
Just text BLUSHING to 22828.

www.ingramcontent.com/pod-product-compliance
Lightning Source LLC
LaVergne TN
LVHW020637100826
845148LV00012B/2216

* 9 7 8 1 6 3 9 5 4 5 1 9 3 *